THE LAST ᴅ..

"I'm gonna kill you, Clint," Meeker said.

"That's a shame, Jack," Clint said. "We used to be friends."

"We were never friends," Meeker said. "You always thought you was better than me."

"You're crazy, Jack," Clint told him. "You're stark raving mad. Killing you will be a pleasure. It will be like killing a mad dog. Now come on, let's get it over with. Show this town you're not a coward. Go for those pretty pearl-handled guns so I can kill you fair and square."

"You ain't gonna kill me," Meeker said. "I'm gonna kill you."

"Then do it," Clint said.

He could see the indecision on the other man's face.

"I'll put two bullets in you before you even clear the leather, Jack," Clint said slowly, "and you know it."

Meeker was flexing his hands and licking his lips. The perspiration was coming down heavily on his face.

"Now, Jack. Now!"

Meeker moved for his guns . . .

The Gunsmith *series*

J. R. Roberts

Books 127 – 189

For books 1 - 126 go to:
www.speakingvolumes.us

THE GUNSMITH

#135

THE LAST BOUNTY

SPEAKING VOLUMES, LLC
NAPLES, FLORIDA
2016

THE GUNSMITH
#135 THE LAST BOUNTY

ISBN 978-1-61232-738-9

THE GUNSMITH

#135

THE LAST BOUNTY

J.R. ROBERTS

Chapter One

Clint Adams stopped overnight in Little Rock, Colorado, before going on to his friend Jack Meeker's ranch. He was just too tired to continue on, even if it was only for another two hours.

Clint was traveling without his rig this trip, choosing instead to ride Duke and leave the wagon and team behind. His intention, right from the moment he left Labyrinth, Texas, was to visit his friend Jack Meeker. Meeker had a successful ranch going two hours north of Little Rock, and Clint hadn't seen Meeker and his wife, Carol, in a couple of years.

In Little Rock he left Duke off at the livery then carried his rifle and saddlebags to the hotel. Little Rock had changed since his last visit, and from what he could see, it was for the better. The hotel was in the same place, but it had been renovated, with an entire floor added onto it, so that it now

1

stood three stories high. What he saw of the rest of the town on his way to the hotel looked the same, either new or renovated. Little Rock, Colorado, seemed to be growing.

He entered the hotel and approached the desk. The man there was very well-dressed, with every hair in place and a carefully waxed mustache.

"Good evening, sir," the man greeted. "Welcome to Little Rock."

"Thanks."

"Will you be staying with us long?"

"Just overnight," Clint said. The man's demeanor put him off. It was meant to be friendly, but it was much too expansive for that. Instead, it came off as forced, as if behind the man's grin he was instead frowning, hating his job and the people it forced him to cater to.

"Very well," the man said, some of the coldness creeping through. Clint guessed that since he was just to be an overnight guest he was not entitled to the full treatment. The smile had even slipped some. "Please sign the register."

Clint signed, "Clint Adams, Labyrinth, Texas," and handed the pen back.

The clerk turned the book around and read the name. If he recognized it, he gave no indication. That suited Clint just fine.

"You'll have number thirty-one," the man said. "That's up on the third floor." He handed Clint the key.

"Thank you."

"Enjoy your stay."

Clint picked up his rifle and saddlebags and walked up the two flights of stairs to the third floor. As he entered the room he noticed that it was much like any other room in any other hotel. Apparently the management had spent most of its money on the outside of the hotel, and not that much on the inside.

He dropped his gear on the bed and took a moment to decide what to do. His bones were telling him to lie down, but his stomach was telling him to go out and get something to eat. In addition, his dust-coated throat was telling him to go out and find a cold beer. Finally, his hunger and his thirst won out. He turned and left the room.

In the lobby he paused, eyeing the entrance to the dining room. Finally, he decided to simply go to the nearest saloon and get himself the beer his throat needed, and then decide where to go to satisfy his stomach. As he left the hotel he realized that the clerk had never looked up from the desk at him.

He walked two blocks to where he remembered the saloon used to be, but it wasn't there anymore. It had apparently been completely torn down, and in its place stood a new two story building that had not yet been completed.

"Excuse me," Clint said, stopping a man who was passing, "where's the nearest saloon?"

"We got two now," the man said proudly. "The Silver Bullet is up the street a couple of blocks, and the Bent Branch is three blocks the other way."

"Which would you suggest?" Clint asked.

"Me? I like the Silver Bullet. It's got prettier girls."

"Does it have cold beer?"

"Cold enough to freeze your teeth, mister!"

"Then the Silver Bullet it is," Clint said. "Thanks very much."

"Enjoy it."

As the man walked away Clint thought that he should have asked him for a good place to eat, but there were other people to ask.

He walked up the street to the Silver Bullet and stopped in front. The building was almost brand new, having lost just a bit of its sheen. It had probably been open about a year. The windows, however, still shone brightly and were multicolored, almost like the stained glass windows in a church. Clint shook his head and entered. Instead of batwing doors there were two more conventional doors side by side. He entered through one, leaving the other closed.

Inside he found himself in a large, high-ceilinged room. There were tables as far as the eye could see, and all the way up front there was a stage. The bar was off to the left, and it ran the entire length of the room. There were *two* bartenders working. It was early evening, and yet both men were busy. Most of the tables looked as if they were taken. Moving about the room were four . . . five . . . no, *six* girls, and from what Clint could see they were all remarkably pretty, and of an age. None of them looked to be over thirty and one—passing very near him at that moment—looked all of eighteen.

He walked to the bar and tried to catch the attention of the nearest bartender, a young man with slicked-down hair, parted down the center.

"Help ya?" the bartender asked.

"A beer."

"Comin' up."

When it came the glass was frosty and the beer so cold it—as promised—almost froze his teeth. He drank half of it down, to the great satisfaction of his throat.

When Clint had finished his beer, the bartender came over and asked, "Just get into town?"

"That's right."

"Well, second one's on the house for newcomers," the man said. "Our way of saying welcome."

"Start pouring, then," Clint said, pushing the glass across the bar to the man. The bar top had an impossible shine to it.

The bartender brought the second beer back, and Clint asked, "Where can I get something good to eat?"

"Right here," the man said. "We make the best steak in town."

Clint looked around for an empty table.

"Don't worry," the man said, as if reading his mind. "We'll get you a table to sit and eat at."

"All right, then," Clint said, "bring me a steak."

"With everything?"

Clint almost asked what "everything" was, then decided to let it be a surprise.

"With everything," he said.

"Comin' up," the bartender said. He waved his arm, and one of the girls appeared. She was tall and slender, with long dark hair and large breasts. She appeared to be in her late twenties.

"Show the gentleman to a table, Harry," the bartender said. "He's got dinner comin'."

"Sure thing," Harry said. She turned and smiled at Clint. He started to pick up his beer, but she got to it before him and said, "I'll take that. Just follow me, honey."

And he did, with pleasure.

Chapter Two

"Did he call you Harry?" Clint asked as she led him to a table in the rear of the room. He hadn't noticed earlier, but there seemed to be a bank of tables against the wall that were empty. They probably reserved them for people who wanted to eat. At the moment, though, no one was eating. He would be the only one.

"That's right," she said, "Harry. My name's Harriet, but I hate that name, so everyone calls me Harry. Here's your table."

She set the beer down on the table and waited for him to sit down. He did so, with his back to the wall.

"I'll bring your dinner when it's ready," she said, "and anything else you might want."

"Thanks," he said.

She gave him another smile—a real one, not

one like the hotel clerk's—and then turned and strutted away. She had a bouncy walk, like some-one with boundless energy. He wondered if he had ever had that much energy, even when he was much younger—like her age.

He nursed his beer until Harry appeared with a plate heaped with food. In addition to a huge steak, there were onions and potatoes, each in excess. She set the plate down in front of him proudly and then produced a knife and fork for him.

"Is there anything else I can get you?" she asked. "Another beer?"

"No," he said, "I still have half of this one, but you can bring me a pot of coffee."

"A whole pot?"

"Yep," he said, "a whole pot."

She put her hand firmly on his shoulder and said, "I'll be right back."

He applied his knife and fork to the mound of food and found everything hot and delicious. She returned fairly quickly with the pot of coffee and a cup.

"There," she said, putting them on the table. "Are you all set now?"

"All set," he said. "Thanks, Harry."

"What's *your* name?" she asked. "I mean, since you know mine, already."

"Clint."

"Will you be in town long?"

"Probably just overnight," he said.

"That's too bad."

"I'll be visiting some friends who live near here, though."

"Well," Harry said, "that means that you might even get back in here again."

"I might," he said. "I might at that."

"Eat hearty, Clint," she said. "I've got to get back to work. It's a busy night."

"Any particular reason?" he asked.

"Oh," she said, "it's busy *every* night, and yes, there is a reason. It's Danielle."

"Danielle?" he asked. "One of the other girls who works here?"

"Oh, she's a girl, all right," Harry said, putting her hands on her hips, "and she works here, all right, but she's sure not just one of the other girls. She performs, up on stage." She waved her arm at the stage in front of the room, in case he hadn't noticed it.

"I see," Clint said. "Is she good?"

"Well," Harry said, "the *men* like her, and that's what counts, ain't it? I'll see you later."

Her tone of voice clearly implied that while the men liked her, the women didn't. In Clint's experience that meant that Danielle was either very beautiful, or flashy, or even both.

Clint was halfway through his meal when he found out that he was right. She *was* both.

Chapter Three

He was pouring himself another cup of coffee when the piano player started playing and a woman who had to be Danielle came out onto the stage to sing. She was tall, with red curls cascading down from her head past her shoulders, which were creamy white—as was her ample bosom. Clint could see why she was a favorite with the men and not with the women. Most of the men seemed more intent on her bouncing breasts than on her singing.

From where he was seated he couldn't really see her face clearly, but his best guess would have made her over thirty. Chances were good that the hair was also a wig. She knew how to present herself, though, and the crowd of appreciative males was making their pleasure known as loudly as they could. By the time she reached the end of her song, she couldn't even be heard over the din. When she finished, the men stamped their feet, clapped their hands, and whistled until she started another song. No slow ballads for this lady, though. If she tried to perform slow songs she'd have to depend solely on her voice to carry the day. Instead, she chose songs with a fast tempo, so that she'd be sure to bring her breasts into play.

After the second song she blew kisses at the audience, executed one single bow designed to show as much of her breasts as she could without having them fall out, and then got off the stage.

The audience shouted for more, but when it became clear that no more was coming they finally settled down and went back to what they were doing before Danielle had come out on stage.

Clint was finishing his meal when Harry came walking over to him.

"What did you think of Danielle?" she asked.

"She certainly knows how to put on a show," he said.

"Did she win you over as an ardent fan, then?" the brunette asked.

"No," he said, "but you will if you bring me some more coffee."

She gave him a sly smile as she picked up the empty pot and said, "There are other ways I'd like to win *you* over, my friend."

He watched her walk away, her saucy behind twitching this way and that, and said, "I'll bet you could do it, too."

•   •   •

She brought him some more coffee, which he drank at his leisure. As busy as the place had been when he walked in, it had gotten even busier—even more crowded than it had been for Danielle's performance.

Gaming tables had opened around the room, making available faro, blackjack, roulette, and poker. In the corner a cage had opened to sell chips. The Silver Bullet did a brisk business, to say the least, and while it might have only been a minor attraction in San Francisco among all the large casinos and hotels in Portsmouth Square, here it was certainly a *major* attraction, not only to Little Rock, but probably the surrounding area, as well.

Harry came over to retrieve his empty cup and pot and asked, "What do you plan to do now?"

"Well," he said, "when I got to town my plan was to eat, drink, and then sleep."

"You've done two of them," she said. "What about the third?"

"I seem to be pretty awake at the moment," he said. "I could probably use a bath, as well."

"You could take a bath and then come back here again," she said. "There's plenty of time."

"Uh, does Danielle do another show later?"

"She does," Harry said. "At eight."

"Then maybe I'll come back at nine," he said. "That is, if I'm still awake."

"Plan on being awake until late," Harry said to him. "I think I can promise you that it will be worth it."

She walked away, long legs flashing in black stockings, her firm butt twitching some more, and he had no doubt that they were both thinking the same thing.

Chapter Four

Clint went back to the hotel and made arrangements with the hotel clerk for a bath. He went upstairs to get a fresh shirt, a fresh pair of jeans, and fresh socks—the only extras he had along with him—and when he returned, a hot bath was waiting for him.

Reclining in the hot water made the tiredness come back, and he was sorely tempted to go right from the tub to his hotel bed. Thoughts of Harry, though, kept intruding on those plans. She was tall and slender—maybe too slender, truth be told—but she had a nice, taut behind and good, firm breasts. She also had a handsome face, with high cheekbones and a nose that might have been too big, but somehow wasn't. In fact, if you took her features separately, they didn't seem to belong on the same face at all. She had large eyes and a small mouth, but she also knew how to apply

14

her makeup. The end result was a face that was rather arresting. Top it all off with a very good personality—and a rather unveiled promise—and she was certainly well worth staying awake for.

He got out of the bath, dried himself off, and dressed in his fresh clothes. Outside he asked the clerk if he could have his dirty clothes cleaned, and the man said he'd have someone come up to the room to pick them up.

The way the man spoke to him—with disdain—finally got to Clint, and he plopped the dirty clothes down on the desk in front of him hard enough to kick up a small cloud of trail dust.

"Hey!" the man said, fanning the air with his hand.

"Why don't I just leave them with you, and you can take care of them?" Clint said.

The man stared at Clint for a moment, opened his mouth as if to speak, and then quickly thought better of it as he saw the look on Clint's face.

"Uh, all right," he finally said, "very well . . . uh, sir . . . I'll have them taken care of."

"And have them taken to my room after they're clean," Clint said.

"Of course, s-sir," the clerk said. "After all, we are h-here to please you."

Clint pointed his finger at the man and said, "Remember you said that." Then he turned and left the hotel.

By the time Clint had reached the Silver Bullet he had calmed down some. He knew it was foolish to let the man get to him, but he disliked bad manners and felt there was no good reason for them.

He walked to the bar and ordered a beer from the same bartender as earlier, then sipped it while scanning the room, looking for Harry. When he didn't see her, he called the bartender over.

"Where's Harry?" he asked.

The man looked around and said, "She was here earlier. She must be in the back—uh, talking to the boss."

The man's pregnant pause did not escape Clint's notice.

"What's that supposed to mean?" he asked.

"Nothin'."

"You trying to tell me something without telling me something?" Clint asked.

"Not really," the man said, wiping at the bar listlessly with a rag. "It's just that—well, Harry would kill me for tellin' you this . . ."

"For telling me what?"

"She's sort of the boss's favorite."

"Does that mean that she gets special treatment?"

"Sometimes."

"And she doesn't have to do what the other girls have to do?"

"Well . . . not always. . . ."

"So you're telling me that she's in the back taking care of the boss right now?"

"Look, mister," the man said, "I'm saying she's *probably* in the back with the boss. If she is, I don't know for sure what they're doin'. She could be gettin' bawled out for all I know."

"Or fired?"

"Uh, no," the man said, "that's one thing she *wouldn't* get. That is . . ."

"*Now* what are you trying to say?" Clint asked impatiently.

"Well, if she was in the back taking care of the boss, and Danielle walked in on them, there'd be hell to pay."

"Ah, Danielle and the boss—say, what's this boss's name, anyway?"

"His name's Ken Becker."

"So Danielle and Mr. Becker have an understanding, huh?"

"Danielle thinks so," the bartender said. "Uh, hey, there's Harry now."

Clint turned and saw Harry coming through a door just to the left of the stage.

"Where's that door go?"

"Backstage," the bartender said. "There's a dressing room back there, some storage . . . and Mr. Becker's office."

"I see."

If she had recently been taking care of the boss, she certainly didn't look it. Every hair was still in place, and as she approached him, smiling broadly, he could see that her makeup was perfect.

"You came back," she said, and then looked at the bartender. "What's Lenny been telling you?"

"Just a little history. . . ." Clint said.

"Lenny!" she said, giving the man a hard stare.

"Uh, I got customers to take care of," Lenny said and hurried away.

"I'll kill him."

"He said you might."

"But that didn't stop him from talking, did it?" she asked. "Did he tell you something about me and Ken Becker?"

"Just that you might be—"

"Well, I'm not," she said. "Ken Becker may think that I am, and Danielle may think that I am, but I'm here to tell you that I'm not. Understand?"

"Sure, Harry, sure," Clint said, liking her more and more. "I understand perfectly."

She took a moment to compose herself and then said, "I've got to get back to work."

"Sure."

She started to walk away, then turned and said to him, "Don't go away, huh?"

"I'll be around," he said. "I promise."

Chapter Five

Clint spent most of the evening watching the action at the tables. The dealers seemed like competent men. The only poker game going was a house game, so he didn't sit in on it. He preferred a poker game where you weren't playing against the house bias. Poker was usually the only game in a casino where you *could* play without going against the house—that is, if there was a private game going.

It was the poker game that he ended up watching, though, because that was what he preferred to play himself. He watched the dealer carefully, because even with the usual house advantage the man seemed to be pulling some amazing cards. Once, the dealer beat kings full with aces full. Had that happened to Clint in a house-operated game he would have gotten up and left. Instead, the player remained in the game, throwing good money after bad.

It was close to midnight when Clint was standing at the bar nursing another beer. The crowd had thinned some, and the bartenders were not quite as busy as they had been earlier. The bartender he had spoken to earlier, Lenny, was leaning against the bar, cleaning some glasses, when he straightened up all of a sudden. Clint turned to see why and saw a man approaching the bar. He looked to be in his mid to late thirties, tall, with a head of bushy black hair and a black mustache to match. He was wearing a suit that cost more than all the clothes Clint had worn in the last two months.

"Ken Becker?" Clint asked the bartender.

"Yup," Lenny said, before Becker reached them. "Evenin', Mr. Becker."

"Hello, Lenny," Becker said. "How'd we do at the bar tonight?"

"Real good, Mr. Becker," Lenny said, "*real* good."

Clint had seen bartenders and other saloon employees kowtow to their bosses before. Hell, he'd seen plenty of employees do it to his friend Rick Hartman, who owned Rick's Place in Labyrinth, Texas. What he was seeing now, though, was more than that. Lenny looked as if he was actually afraid of Becker.

"That's fine, Lenny," Becker said. "Have you, uh, noticed our friend Harry tonight?"

"Uh, sure, Mr. Becker," Lenny said. "I see her every night."

"No," Becker said, becoming impatient. "I mean have you seen her giving anyone any *special* attention tonight?"

"Uh," Lenny said, his eyes flicking briefly to Clint and then back to his boss. Clint didn't think Becker had even noticed. "Uh, no, Mr. Becker, I ain't seen nothin' like that tonight."

"Uh-huh," Becker said, thoughtfully. "Well, just keep an eye on her for me, Lenny, there's a good man."

"Sure, Mr. Becker, sure thing," Lenny said.

Becker turned to leave and saw Clint standing nearby.

"New in town?" he asked.

"Just got in today," Clint said.

"Are you enjoying yourself here?"

"You have a fine place here, Mr. Becker," Clint said, "a very fine place."

"Good, glad to hear it," Becker said. "Do any gambling?"

"I do some," Clint said, "but not here."

Becker frowned at that, not sure he had heard right.

"What's the matter with gambling here? Don't you have confidence in your luck?"

"When I gamble," Clint said, "I don't rely on luck to win, Mr. Becker."

"What's your game?" Becker asked.

"Poker."

"We have a poker game going—"

"I've seen your poker game," Clint said, "and your dealer."

"Don't want to try your, uh, hand?"

"Not against him."

Becker grinned tightly and said, "Is he too good for you?"

Clint sipped his beer, wondered if he should be honest with the man, then decided, why not?

"He cheats."

Out of the corner of his eye Clint saw Lenny cringe. Becker stared at Clint for a few moments, his face expressionless, before speaking.

"What?"

"I said," Clint repeated, "he cheats."

"I don't believe it."

"Oh, he's very good at it," Clint said, "and he doesn't do it very often. He picks his spots— and they're good spots. Still, giving yourself aces full to beat someone's kings full is a little obvious."

Becker turned and looked in the direction of the poker table.

"No," Clint said, looking past him, "not that dealer. The one before him."

"Kyle," Becker said.

"I think I heard someone call him that."

Becker eyed Clint for a moment, then asked, "Why should I believe you?"

"Don't," Clint said, shrugging. "It doesn't matter to me. As long as I know you have a dealer who cheats, I won't play here."

"I could watch him myself," Becker said.

"If you do that," Clint said, "he won't cheat."

"Then how do I confirm what you've told me?"

"You'll have to have someone watch him," Clint said, "someone he doesn't know, but someone you trust."

"Like you?" Becker asked. "You angling for a job?"

"Number one," Clint said, seeing that Harry had come over to within earshot, "I didn't come here looking for a job; number two, even if I was, why should you hire me after I've already told you what he was doing for nothing?"

"You're right," Becker said. "All right, yes, I'll have someone watch him, and if I find out the little weasel is cheating—I run clean games, Mr.—"

"Adams," Clint said, "Clint Adams."

Now when Becker stared at Clint his face was anything but expressionless.

"Clint *Adams*?"

"That's right."

"All right," the man said, after a moment, "all right. Are you going to be in town long?"

"Not long," Clint said. "I'll be visiting some friends north of town, though."

"If it turns out you're right," Becker said, "I'm going to want to thank you."

"Well," Clint said, "if you get your confirmation pretty quick, maybe I'll still be around."

"Lenny," Becker said, "give the man a beer, on the house."

"Thank you," Clint said.

Becker turned to leave, looked over his shoulder at Clint one last time, then walked away without giving Harry a glance. He walked all the way to the front and went through the door to the left of the stage.

"Here's your beer," Lenny said.

"Thanks."

"Jesus," Lenny said, "when you told him Kyle was cheatin', I didn't know what to expect."

"Why, Lenny?" Clint asked. "Why are you afraid of him?"

"You kiddin'?" Lenny asked. "He's my boss."

"That means you have to respect him," Clint said, "and give him a good day's work. I want to know why you're *afraid* of him."

"Because . . ." Lenny said, "because he's . . . he's Mr. *Becker*. 'Scuse me, I got work to do."

Clint watched the man move to the other end of the bar and then looked at Harry, who was sidling up next to him.

"You don't know who Becker is, do you?" she asked.

"I never heard of him," he admitted.

"Finish your beer," she said. "We'll go someplace where we can talk, and I'll tell you all about him."

"I'd rather hear all about you," Clint said.

"Don't worry, honey," she said, putting her arm in his, "you're gonna know everything about me you want to know."

Chapter Six

A few hours later Clint was thinking he might not know all there was to know about Harry, or all he would want to know, but he had seen all there was to see about her. That much was for sure.

On the way to the hotel she had explained how Ken Becker was the driving force behind the rebirth of Little Rock.

"He came to town, brought money with him, brought in new ideas—"

"Like the Silver Bullet?"

"Especially the Silver Bullet," she said. "Because of him, Little Rock is gonna end up on the map."

"Like Denver?"

"Maybe like a small Denver," she said. "Hell, you said you have friends here. That means you know what this place was like a few years ago."

25

"Five or six," he corrected.

"No difference," she said. "It only changed a couple of years ago when Ken Becker arrived."

"From where?"

She thought a moment, then shrugged.

"Nobody knows, really," she said. "Maybe San Francisco?"

"Given what he's done with the Silver Bullet, that's certainly a possibility," Clint said.

"You've been to San Francisco?" she asked.

"Quite a few times."

"I've never been there," she said. "I'd love to go."

"So go."

"Yeah," she said, "sure."

When they reached the hotel and entered, the desk clerk looked up and blinked when he saw Clint. He watched as Clint and Harry walked to the steps and started up.

"What did you do to him?" she asked.

"We had a small attitude problem," he said, "but we straightened it out."

"Oh yeah," she said. "I can see that."

Clint unlocked the door to his room, and Harry went in ahead of him. He turned up the flame on the gas lamp behind the door.

"I've never been up here on the third floor," she said, taking off her wrap. She was still wearing her low-cut saloon gown. "They didn't change the rooms, did they?"

"Like most people," he said, "they changed what other people could see."

She folded her arms beneath her breasts and stared at him.

"What's that mean?"

He looked at her and said, "Just that what's on the outside isn't always what's on the inside."

"I hope I'm not supposed to know what that means," she said.

"Look at it this way," he said. "On the outside you're a beautiful, vibrant, desirable woman. What are you on the inside?"

She smiled and said, "What you see is what you get."

"But not all the time," he said, "not with everybody. What do you see when you look at me?"

She studied him for a few moments, then said, "A sad man."

"What?"

"Well, you asked," she said. "I see a good-looking man who's just a little bit sad about the way his life has gone."

He hesitated a moment and then said, "This isn't working." She had described him perfectly after a very short acquaintance. She was either a good guesser or very intuitive.

"Pick another example," she suggested.

"Okay," he said. "Your boss, Becker. When I look at him, I see a confident, successful businessman."

"And he is."

"But what's he like on the inside?" Clint asked.

"Believe me," she said, "you don't want to know . . . and I don't want to talk about him anymore."

"All right," he said. "What do you want to talk about?"

She moved closer to him and put her hands on his chest, then started to unbutton his shirt.

"I don't want to talk at all," she said. She slid her hands inside his shirt and rubbed her palms over his nipples. "I'm through talkin'. Now I just want to go and go."

He put his arms around her and said, "Then let's go," just before kissing her. . . .

Now he was staring down at her while she slept. She looked much younger than he had first guessed. Maybe when she was awake—and at work—it was her confident demeanor that made her seem older than she was. He now guessed that she was about twenty-three or four.

It was warm in the room, and the sheet was gathered down around her waist. She had remarkably large, firm breasts for a woman who was otherwise very thin. He could see the outline of her ribs as she reclined on her back. Beneath the sheet her long, slender legs were outlined, as well. Her breasts were flattened only slightly, the brown nipples very soft and flat. He leaned over and touched the tip of his tongue to her left nipple and then watched it tighten, harden, and extend. He did the same to the right one, and she started to moan. She stretched, moving her legs, then reached for his head and cradled it while he sucked her nipple into his mouth.

"Mmmm, more?" she said.

"Yes," he said, "more. . . ."

He slid one leg over her, then straddled her and touched the tip of his hard penis to her moist portal.

"Yes," she said. She reached for his buttocks with both hands and pulled him to her. He penetrated her cleanly, drove in to the hilt, and just stayed there.

"Oooh, you feel good," she said.

"And you," he said in her ear, "are so hot, like fire. . . ."

"I am on fire," she said.

"And you want me to put it out?" he asked.

She laughed, a sound that started deep in her throat, and said, "Hell no, honey, I want you to fan it. . . ."

Chapter Seven

When he woke the next morning *she* was fanning *his* flame. She was down between his legs, working on him with her mouth. She peppered his inner thighs with warm, wet kisses, then worked her tongue along the length of him, fondling his testicles with one hand. As her tongue moved up, her other hand encircled him at the base of his cock. Finally, she reached the head and wet it thoroughly with her tongue before enveloping him with her hot, avid mouth. He reached down to cup her head and kept his eyes closed as she sucked hard, moving her head faster and faster.

"What do you have planned for the rest of the day?" she asked later.

He sat up and swung his feet to the floor.

"I came here to visit some friends," he said. "I guess that's what I'll do."

"Oh, that's right," she said, running one finger down his spine, "you mentioned that, didn't you?"

"Besides," he said, "don't you have to rest? You were working late last night, and didn't get much rest here."

"Yeah," she said, "I guess I should get some sleep, otherwise I'll start to look my age."

"Your age?" he said. "You can't be more than . . . twenty-three?"

She sat up, put her arms around him, and kissed the back of his neck. Her breasts were pressed tightly against his back.

"You're a sweet man, did you know that?"

"Actually," he said, kissing one of her arms, "I've been told that before."

She leaned away from him and slapped his shoulder.

"I'll bet."

He stood up and started to wash, using the basin and bowl on the dresser.

"You can stay here if you want."

"No, that's all right," she said. "I'll go back to my own bed."

She came up behind him and pressed herself to him.

"That is, if you're through with me?"

"Oh, I'm through with you, all right," he said, "for now."

•   •   •

They left the hotel together, Harry heading for her room and Clint for the livery. When he arrived there was no one around, so he went inside to saddle Duke himself. He had thrown the blanket over the big gelding's back when Duke shifted his position and snorted.

"Easy, boy," Clint said in the big horse's ear. "I know we're not alone."

He lifted the saddle onto Duke's back and was cinching it tight when the first man stepped into view.

"Can I help you?" Clint asked. "Liveryman's not here right now. If you want your horse, you'll have to do what I'm doing, saddle your own."

"I ain't here for a horse," the man said. "I'm here to deliver a message."

"Oh yeah?" Clint said. He turned to face the man. He was wearing well-worn clothes, and the gun and holster on his hip looked like they'd seen a lot of use, too. Clint didn't know him. He had to be hired muscle, but hired by whom? "What's the message?"

"Stay away from Miss Bonner."

"Is that all?" Clint asked. "Sure, just tell me one thing."

"What?"

"Who's Miss Bonner?"

"Harry," the man said. "Harriet Bonner."

"Oh," Clint said, "Harry? Sorry, I can't do it."

"This is a warning."

"Fine," Clint said. "I'll take it as a warning, then. Thanks."

The man looked confused.

"That mean you'll stay away from her?"

"No," Clint said, "it means you delivered your warning, and I heard you."

The man was growing more confused by the minute.

"Then you ain't gonna stay away from her?"

"Ah . . . I don't think so, no."

"See?" another voice said. "I told you. You gotta do more than just talk."

Another man stepped into view then. Like the first man everything he had on he'd been wearing for some time, without washing it. He was as tall as his cohort, but a little broader in the chest and shoulders. Clint guessed that this man believed in being more physical with his warnings.

"This a friend of yours?" Clint asked the first man.

"We work together."

"Giving out warnings?"

"And more," the second man said.

"Well, this has been nice," Clint said, "but if you guys will step aside, me and my horse will be going."

"We can't do that," the second man said.

"Why not?"

"We got to make sure that you're warned good and proper."

"Let me guess," Clint said. "That means I've got to come out of this with some bruises, right?"

"A lot of bruises," the first man said, "and maybe a broken bone or two."

"That's your idea of a warning?" Clint asked.

The second man nodded and said, "That's it."

"No," Clint said, "that's not it. Go!" He slapped Duke on the rump, and the big horse shot forward. The two men were too startled to get out of the way, and the big horse ran right into them, knocking them both over.

Clint came out of the stall right behind Duke. He quickly disarmed the first man while he lay on the floor. As he went for the second man's gun, the man took a wild swing at him from the ground. Clint hit him once in the jaw, then took the man's gun and flung it into the hayloft.

The first man seemed content to stay on his ass, but the second man shook his head and started to come off the ground at Clint.

"If you get up," Clint said to him, "I'm gonna have to hurt you."

"Try it without your horse," the bigger man said, coming to his feet.

Clint gave him no time to get set. He kicked out with the heel of his boot and came into contact with the man's knee. The force of the blow caused the man's legs to bend the wrong way, and he screamed and went down, holding the damaged leg.

"I told you," Clint said to him. He turned to the first man, who put his hands out in a gesture of surrender. "Tell your boss you delivered your warning."

"I'll tell him."

Clint followed Duke, who had run outside and

was waiting for him. He didn't bother asking the two men who they worked for. He felt that the answer was much too obvious to even warrant asking the question.

Chapter Eight

When Clint saw the ranch he frowned. He remembered the Meeker place as a small but well-maintained ranch, and he was looking at anything but that. The house looked the same, except that it was in dire need of a paint job. The corral was in a state of disrepair, as was the barn, but the thing that really concerned Clint was that the corral was empty. He couldn't remember a time when there weren't horses in the corral. Jack Meeker was a genius with horses. He raised them, trained them; there was a time when he raced them. He could do anything he wanted to with a horse.

What the hell had happened?

As he rode up to the house, his sense of smell told him that some things didn't change. Carol Meeker was one of the best cooks he had ever encountered, and he had never been here when he couldn't smell something cooking, as he did now.

He dismounted, stepped up onto the porch, and knocked on the door. He heard footsteps from inside and then the door swung inward.

"Well I'll be—" Jack Meeker said.

"Hello, Jack."

"Clint!"

Meeker was not a big man, but from years of dealing with animals who weighed over a thousand pounds, he was very strong. He stepped forward and grabbed Clint in a bear hug, lifting him off his feet.

"Carol! Look who's here!" he shouted, right into Clint's ear.

"Put me down, you big ox!" Clint yelled. "You're breaking my back."

Jack Meeker put Clint back on his feet and stepped backward.

"Let me take a good look at you, son," he said. He frowned, studying the friend he hadn't seen in some years, and then said, "Jesus, you've got old!"

"He has not," Carol Meeker said. "Move out of the way, Jack. Clint, how wonderful to see you."

Carol Meeker had changed. To Clint she had always been a slightly plump, very comfortable-looking woman. The years had been very kind to her—so kind, in fact, that she had apparently lost a lot of weight, which had changed her from a comfortable-looking woman into a fine-looking one. He couldn't believe the change losing some weight had made in her.

She put her arms around him and hugged him tightly, her still generous bosom pressed against his chest. *That* hadn't changed.

"Carol," he said, as she stepped back, "you're beautiful."

"Ain't she, though?" Meeker said, beaming proudly, then a cloud passed over his face and he said, "That's about the *only* good thing that's happened in a while."

"Jack," Carol said warningly. "Have you had breakfast?" she asked Clint, before he had a chance to ask Meeker to explain what he meant.

"Of course I haven't," he said. "I knew I was coming here."

"Well, come on in and eat," she said. "Jack, step back and let Clint in."

"Come on, come on," Meeker said, moving back, "come on in and strap on the feed bag, old son."

Clint stepped inside. The interior of the house was just about as he remembered it, still neat, tidy, and modest. Most of the furniture that was in the house had been built by Jack Meeker, himself. He was almost as good with a hammer and saw as he was with horses.

"Sit," Carol said, bringing a pot of coffee to the table with two cups. "Have some coffee while I get breakfast finished."

Meeker poured two cups of coffee and asked, "How you been, son?"

"I've been fine, Jack," Clint said. Meeker had always called him "son," even though the man was actually a couple of years younger than he was.

"So tell me," Meeker said, slapping Clint on the shoulder, "what brings you here?"

"You want the truth?" Clint asked.

"Yes," Meeker said.

"Of course we do," Carol said.

"I came to see you and Carol."

"Hogwash."

"I believe him," Carol said. She came to the table with two plates heaped with eggs, potatoes, and bacon. "Clint wouldn't lie about a thing like that." She leaned over and kissed Clint on the cheek. "And I'm happy that you did come to see us."

"Thanks, Carol," he said.

"Go on, dig in," she said. "I remember how you like to eat."

"I like to eat when *you* cook, Carol," he said. "Aren't you going to eat, too?"

"Look at me, Clint Adams," she said. "Do I look like I eat as much as I used to?"

"You look . . . wonderful," he said.

As she went back to the stove, Clint leaned over and said to Meeker, "What did you do to her?"

"She did it to herself," Meeker said in normal tone. "Said she was tired of looking *comfortable*."

"Comfortable?" Clint frowned, wondering if he'd ever said that himself out loud.

"Ah, somebody in town made the comment," Meeker said. "Right then and there she swore to lose weight, and she did. Me, I kind of liked it when there was a lot more of her to love."

"Oh, sure," Carol said from the stove. "I lost weight, and he became as randy as an old goat.

He never leaves me alone, now. That tells you how much he liked me when I was fat."

In unison Clint and Meeker both said, "You were never fat!"

She laughed and said, "You're both a couple of old sweethearts."

She did sit with them, however, and have coffee, and the two of them pumped Clint to tell them what he had been doing since they had last seen him. Clint answered their questions, but had the uncomfortable feeling that they were questioning him so intensely so that he wouldn't question them.

He decided that he was just going to have to get Jack Meeker by himself later and find out what the hell had happened to them since the last time he was here.

Chapter Nine

They talked for a while inside, and then Carol waved them out of the house so she could clean up.

Outside Clint said, "I have some questions, Jack."

"I thought you might," Meeker said. "I think I know what they are."

"What the hell happened?"

"See? I was right."

"Can you tell me?"

"I wish I could, Clint."

"What do you mean ?"

"I mean . . . it all just sort of dried up," Meeker said. He flopped his arms around helplessly. "The army found a new source for their horses and stopped buying from me. My business just seemed to dry up and blow away. The place is falling apart, and I don't have the money to make the proper

41

repairs. I have just enough to keep us going, but that's not going to last long."

"What about a loan?"

"I'm going into town today, to the bank," Meeker said.

"I meant a loan from me."

"Never," Meeker said.

"Jack, we're friends—"

"I don't borrow money from friends, Clint," Meeker said. "I don't want to hear any more about it."

"Well . . . all right, but I'll ride along into town with you."

"You just rode *out* from town."

"That's okay," Clint said. "Duke can use the exercise."

"You stayin' at the hotel?"

"Yeah."

"Okay, then we can pick up your stuff while we're there," Meeker said. "You'll be staying out here with us for a while."

"Jack, I don't want to impose," Clint said. "I mean, if things are rough—"

"When things get so rough I can't offer a friend the hospitality of my home, I'll pack it in for good," Meeker said. "Come on, we'll saddle the horses and get into town. I'm sure the bank manager is anxiously waiting to turn me down."

Clint had never seen Jack Meeker with such a defeated attitude. He didn't like the way it looked. He hoped that the bank manager wouldn't turn Meeker down, because then he'd have to once again broach the subject of a loan, and he knew that would make Meeker angry.

They promised Carol they'd be home in time for dinner and rode off toward town.

"How about letting me buy you a drink before you go to the bank?" Clint asked when they arrived. "It'll fortify you."

"Okay," Meeker said, "a drink I'll take from you."

"Good. We'll go over to the Silver Bullet."

Meeker stiffened a bit and then said, "If that's what you want. You're buying."

They left the horses in front of the Silver Bullet and went inside. There was only one bartender behind the bar at this time of the day, and it was Lenny.

"Back for more?" Lenny asked. Clint wondered if the bartender knew what had happened that morning in the livery, or if he was simply referring to drinks.

"Two beers," Clint said.

"You've been here before," Meeker said.

"Once or twice."

"When did you get to town again?"

"Yesterday."

"Why'd you pick this place?"

"It was the closest saloon to the hotel," Clint said, as Lenny served them their beers. "Why? Don't you like this place?"

"The place is all right," Meeker said. "It's the owner I'm not crazy about."

Lenny, hearing this, moved away from the two men quickly.

"Have you got a beef with Becker?"

"Becker's got a ranch east of town," Meeker said. "He's the one the army's buying horses from now."

"Oh," Clint said, "I see."

"He's a big man hereabouts," Meeker said.

"I heard he brought some fresh money into town," Clint said.

"Oh, sure," Meeker said. "Lots of people give him credit for Little Rock's new prosperity—that is, people whose business he hasn't ruined."

"I don't understand."

"He's opened up businesses all over town— all over the county—in direct competition with others, like me . . . and the others—like me— just can't compete, so we're falling by the way-side."

Clint didn't comment. It sounded like Becker was a good businessman, and he couldn't fault the man for that. He could, however, fault him for sending two men after him in the livery that morning.

"Well," Clint said, "if it's any consolation to you, Becker and I haven't exactly gotten off on the right foot, either."

"What happened between the two of you?"

"Well, for one thing I told him his poker dealer was cheating."

"And was he?"

"He sure was."

"I'll bet he didn't like that," Meeker said. "Getting caught, I mean."

"He seemed angry," Clint said.

"I'll say."

"I mean, he claimed to run a clean house."

"Sure he did," Meeker said. "What else would he claim? Is that all?"

"No," Clint said. "It seems I made friends with a lady he, uh, has his eyes on."

"You met Danielle?" Meeker asked, surprised.

"No, not Danielle," Clint said. "A gal named Harry."

"Ah," Meeker said, "Harry. . . . I see."

"That's not all," Clint said. He told Meeker how he had been threatened by the two men in the livery that morning.

"You *have* managed to make a lot of friends in a short period of time, haven't you?" Meeker asked.

"Actually," Clint said, "there's probably one other person I should meet if I'm going to be around here for a while."

"And who's that?"

"The sheriff," Clint said.

Chapter Ten

When they left the saloon they split up. Meeker was going to the bank, and Clint was going to the sheriff's office.

"In case anything else happens," Clint said, "I want the local law to know that I didn't come to town looking for any trouble."

"Don't sound like a bad idea," Meeker said. He dried his palms on his thighs. "Wish me luck. I don't think I was this nervous when I asked Carol to marry me."

"Haven't you ever taken out a loan before?" Clint asked.

Meeker looked at him. "No."

Clint knew what it must have been taking for his friend to finally ask someone for a loan, even if it was a bank. Jack Meeker had done everything himself all his life. This move was taking a lot of courage, and a lot of pride swallowing.

"Good luck," Clint said sincerely, putting his hand on his friend's shoulder.

"I'll meet you back here," Meeker said. "We'll either drink to celebrate, or drink to drown my sorrows."

"Either way," Clint said, "I'll buy."

Clint watched Meeker walk away, his shoulders slumped as if he were walking his last mile. He turned then and headed for the sheriff's office.

Jack Meeker walked into the bank and approached one of the teller's cages. The teller knew him because he had an account there—an account he had long since almost emptied in an attempt to keep his ranch afloat.

"Hello, Mr. Meeker," the teller said. He was a little man with thinning hair and a well-groomed mustache. Meeker thought his name was Louis, but wasn't sure.

"Hello," Meeker said.

"What can I do for you today?" the man asked. "We haven't seen you here in some time."

"I know," Meeker said. "I'd like to see Mr. Flowers."

"Mr. Flowers?" the man said, frowning.

"Yes, the bank manager?"

"Oh," the teller said, "oh, I see, it *has* been a while since you were here last. Mr. Flowers is no longer the bank manager."

"He isn't?"

"No sir," the man said. "He was replaced several months ago."

"All right, then," Meeker said, "I'd like to see the new manager, whatever his name is."

"Mr. Deavers," the man said. "I'll tell him you're here. Please wait a minute."

Meeker remained there at the teller's cage waiting, and the man returned in precisely one minute.

"Come this way, please."

"Thanks."

Meeker followed the teller to the manager's office.

"Mr. Deavers, this is Mr. Meeker."

"All right, Louis," Deavers said. "Thank you."

"Yes, sir," Louis said, and went back to his cage.

"Come in, Mr. Meeker," Deavers said. "Have a seat."

Meeker entered the room and took a seat across from the bank manager. Deavers was a large, red-faced man who obviousy favored big cigars. There was the stub of one in an ashtray, and the air was thick with the smoke from the one he currently held in his hand. He was bald on top, with a fringe of hair on the sides and in the back, and he had a small, black mustache.

"I'm Harmon Deavers, the bank manager," Deavers said. "I understand you had an account here for some time, but no longer do."

"I still have an account, Mr. Deavers," Meeker said.

Deavers frowned at a piece of paper he had on his desk, then said, "Oh, yes, I see . . . with a balance of five dollars."

"Uh, yes," Meeker said. He was feeling so embarrassed that he wanted to bolt and run.

"Well, how can I help you today, Mr. Meeker?" Deavers asked. He folded his hands across his girth, dropping cigar ash on his vest in the process.

This is it, Meeker thought. It was either ask for a loan or cut and run. . . .

Clint knocked on the door to the sheriff's office and entered, closing the door behind him. For a moment he thought it was empty, but then a man came out from the back, where the cells were. He was tall, about fifty, and stared at Clint curiously.

"Help ya?" he asked.

"You're the sheriff?"

"That's right," the man said. "Sheriff Hays, Del Hays."

"Well, Sheriff," Clint said, "my name is Clint Adams, and I got into town yesterday."

"Oh yeah," the sheriff said, "I know who you are."

"Do you?"

"Sure," the man said, turning to face Clint squarely. "You're the troublemaker."

Obviously, Clint thought, Ken Becker had been here first.

Chapter Eleven

"That's not the way I remember it, Sheriff," Clint said.

"Tell me how you remember it, then," the sheriff invited.

"What did you hear?"

"That you jumped two men this morning and took their guns."

"Did you ever think I might've had a good reason?"

"You're saying you had just cause," the sheriff said, "but even then *I* usually relieve men of their guns when there's a reason."

"You didn't say that the two men worked for Ken Becker," Clint said.

"Oh? Did they?"

"Didn't they?"

The sheriff rubbed his jaw and said, "They

work for him, yeah, but what's that got to do
with—"

"Becker sent them after me to warn me, Sheriff,"
Clint said.

"Warn you about what?"

"To stay away from a certain lady."

"And that's when you jumped them?"

"No," Clint said, "I jumped them when the warning started to get physical."

"How physical?"

"One of them said they were going to give me
some broken bones."

The sheriff moved around behind his desk and
sat down, his arms folded across his chest.

"And *that's* when you jumped them?"

"Yes."

"Adams," Hays said, "I know your reputation
with a gun. Why didn't you just use it?"

"I don't know what you've heard, Sheriff," Clint
said, "but I don't use my gun unless I have to,
and I didn't think that I had to. All I did was
take their guns and give them a message to take
back to their boss."

"Which was?"

"I don't take kindly to warnings."

"Listen, I don't know what's happenin' here between you and Becker," Hays said, "but I don't
want any trouble in my town."

"That's what I came here to tell you," Clint said.
"*I* don't want any trouble. I came here to visit with
some friends, and that's it."

"How'd you get mixed up with Mr. Becker?"

the sheriff asked. It didn't escape Clint's notice that the man said Becker's name with a certain amount of respect.

"I stopped at the Silver Bullet for a drink last night," Clint said.

"And met this, uh, lady?"

"That's right."

"We ain't talkin' about Danielle, are we?"

"No," Clint said, but he didn't offer the name of the lady they were talking about.

"I see," the sheriff said. "Well, I don't have to tell you that Mr. Becker is a pretty important man in this town."

"So I understand."

"It might be smart if you did your drinkin' somewhere else."

"Is that advice?"

"It is," Hays said. "I'd also advise you to stay away from the lady in question."

"That's all?" Clint said. "That's all you have to tell me?"

"Well," Hays said, "it wouldn't hurt none if you left town."

"As it happens," Clint said, "I won't be staying in town, but that doesn't mean I won't be *in* town from time to time."

"That's fine," Hays said. "Just stay away from Mr. Becker, and what's his."

"The lady we're talking about is *not* his."

"He thinks she is," Hays said.

"Sheriff," Clint said, "do you work for Becker or the town?"

Sheriff Hays sat forward in his chair with his chin thrust out belligerently.

"I work for the town, Adams," Hays said, "and I do what's best for the town."

"And keeping Ken Becker happy, that's good for the town, right?"

"Keeping Mr. Becker happy is *very* good for the town," Hays said.

Clint put his hand on the doorknob and said, "Sheriff, I came here to tell you that I'm not looking for trouble."

"Fine," Hays said. "Keep it that way."

Clint wanted to say more, then thought better of it. Obviously, Sheriff Hays simply felt that what was best for Ken Becker was best for the town.

He left and went to find Meeker. If he took the sheriff's "advice," they'd have to do their drinking in a different place.

Chapter Twelve

Clint was approaching the Silver Bullet when he saw Meeker coming from the other direction. From the slump of his shoulders, Clint guessed that his friend had been turned down for the loan. They met almost directly in front of the Silver Bullet.

"Didn't get it?" Clint asked.

Meeker looked at him and said, "Didn't get it."

Clint looked at the front doors of the Silver Bullet and thought, Ah, the hell with it.

"Come on," he said, "I'll buy you a drink. Hell, I'll buy you a lot of drinks."

Maybe if he got Meeker drunk he'd be able to get him to accept a loan.

There were only three other customers in the saloon, two men standing separately at the bar, and one man nodding off over a beer at a table.

Meeker walked to a back table and sat down

while Clint went for the beers.

"I don't think you should be in here," Lenny said as he handed two beers to Clint.

"Don't tell anybody I'm here," Clint said.

"If the boss sees you—"

"If the boss sees me, you send him over to me," Clint said.

"Oh, Jesus . . ." Lenny said, shaking his head.

Clint walked to the table and put a beer down in front of Meeker.

"What happened?"

"They got a new bank manager," Meeker said. "He said I had no money in the bank to speak of so there was no way they could give me a loan."

"But that's why you wanted a loan," Clint said. "Jesus, if you had money you wouldn't need a loan."

"I tried to explain that to him."

"What's wrong with bankers, anyway?"

"Damned if I know."

"What about your ranch?"

"What about it?"

"It must be worth something."

"I'm not going to sell the ranch, Clint."

Clint forgot that Meeker had never taken out a loan before.

"I don't mean sell it; I mean put it up as collateral," he said.

"What the hell does that mean?"

Clint explained that Meeker could take a loan out against the value of the ranch.

"And if I don't pay back the loan?"

"Then the bank takes the ranch."

"That's the same as selling it!"

"No, it's not," Clint said. "You only lose the ranch if you can't pay back the loan."

"Well, what if I can't?"

"What's going to happen if you don't get a loan?"

"I'll lose the ranch."

"So? What's the difference, then?"

Meeker thought it over for the length of time it took him to drink that beer, and a second one.

"You know what?" he said later.

"What?"

"You're right."

"I know I'm right," Clint said. "I mean, I'm right if that's what you want to do."

"It's what I want to do," Meeker said. "I need that loan."

"Okay then. . . ."

"Okay. . . ."

"You want me to go with you?"

"No," Meeker said, "no, I'll go by myself. I don't need nobody to hold my hand."

"Okay," Clint said. "I'll wait here."

"Here?"

"Yeah, what's wrong with here?"

Meeker frowned and asked, "What happened with you and the sheriff?"

"The sheriff is only concerned with keeping Ken Becker happy," Clint said. "He told me to stay away from him."

"And you're here? In his place?"

Clint looked around and said, "Well, I don't see

him here. Look at it this way. Where's the last place Becker would expect me to be?"

Meeker thought a moment and then said, "Here?"

"Right," Clint said. "You go and get your loan, and I'll wait right here."

"That's what I'm gonna do," Meeker said. "I'm gonna go and get that loan."

Clint watched as Meeker weaved his way to the door and wondered if he should be letting the man go over to the bank alone in the condition he was in.

Looking into his beer Clint wondered why the banker himself hadn't suggested to Meeker that he put his place up for collateral.

Chapter Thirteen

Louis, the teller, stared through the cage at the man with the gun.

"You can't really get away with this, you know," he said.

"Shut your mouth and put the money in a sack," the man said.

Louis did as he was told, but this man wasn't particularly good at his job—if, indeed, robbing banks was his chosen vocation. Why, the man hadn't even bothered to put on a mask. That meant he wasn't very smart. Of course, Louis thought, it might also mean that he planned to kill everyone in the bank before he left.

That thought made Louis a little more nervous than he had been up to that point.

"What's going on?" Deavers, the bank manager, asked as he came out of his office.

"We're being held up, Mr. Deavers," Louis said, continuing to put money in the sack he had provided. The thief hadn't even brought his own.

"What do you mean, held up?" Deaver demanded.

"Shut up," the man with the gun said. "You the manager?"

"That's right, and I'd advise you to give this up right—"

"Shut up!" the bank robber said. Louis noted that this seemed to be the man's favorite phrase. "You're gonna open the safe for me."

"I am not," Deavers said.

"You'll do it, or I'll shoot you."

"Shoot me and you'll *never* get into the safe," Deavers reasoned.

"If you won't open it for me, I might as well shoot you," the robber said. "It's all the same to me."

The robber's reasoning made sense to Louis.

"You better do what he says, Mr. Deavers," Louis said. "I think he means it."

Harmon Deavers glared at Louis and the bank robber with equal venom, then turned to the safe and started spinning the dial. He couldn't remember if there was a gun inside or not. If there was, this bank robber was in for a big surprise.

Jack Meeker hurried to the bank, convinced that by putting his ranch up as coll—whatever Clint had said—he was going to get his loan. Even if the ranch wasn't in as good shape as it used to be, it was worth something.

He had no idea that he was about to walk in on a situation that would forever change his life from that moment on.

"Come on, come on," the bank robber said, impatiently waggling his gun. "Put all the money into the sack."

"Hold the sack steady, Louis," Deavers said.

"I'm s-sorry," Louis said. "I-I'm a little nervous."

"Be ready to move, man," Deaver whispered.

"Are we going to run, sir?" Louis asked.

"No," Deavers said, "we're going to jump him when he's not looking."

"Wha—"

"Stop whispering!" the bank robber said. "Don't try anything or you'll both be dead."

There was no one else in the bank except for the three men. One teller had called in sick that morning; another was still out to lunch.

"Is that sack full?" the robber asked.

"Yessir," Louis said, "it's full."

"Give it here, then."

Deavers picked up the sack, but the robber said, "No, not you, the other fella. The little guy."

"Me?" Louis said, his voice a squeak.

"That's right," the robber said, "you."

Louis swallowed hard, then took the sack from Deavers and walked out from behind his cage to give it to the robber.

"Come on, come on," the robber said.

He was a skinny, homely-looking man, not much taller than Louis, himself. The teller was thinking to himself, who was he calling little?

"Here," Louis said, thrusting the bulky sack at the man, who accepted it with one hand.

"Now back up," the robber said.

He's going to shoot us now, Louis thought, backing up until he bumped into the front of his teller's cage.

The man started backing toward the front door, keeping both men covered. It didn't seem as if he were going to shoot them now.

The bank robber had a problem, though. He had his gun in one hand and the sack of money in the other, and he had to open the door. When he reached the door he realized his predicament. He didn't want to put the gun down, or stop covering the two men with it, but he also didn't want to put down the sack of money, now that he had it in his hand.

"Come out from behind there," he told Deavers.

Deavers came out from behind the cage very slowly. Louis, meanwhile, was now convinced that the man *was* going to shoot them, and that there was nothing they could do about it.

"Get on the floor, both of you," the bank robber ordered.

"Now wait just a minute—" Deavers said.

"On your bellies!" the man shouted.

Jesus, the teller thought, he's going to shoot us while we're lying down. Of course, that didn't keep him from dropping to the floor and pressing his nose to it.

Deavers was slower, but eventually he, too, had his nose pressed to the floor . . . and that's when Jack Meeker entered the scene.

Chapter Fourteen

As Meeker got closer to the bank his resolve became stronger and stronger, and he began to quicken his pace. When he finally mounted the boardwalk in front of the bank and got to the door, he grabbed it and opened it almost violently.

Inside, the bank robber, who now had the two bank employees on the floor, was reaching for the door, and as he closed his hand over the doorknob—the hand with which he also held the gun—it was yanked open from the outside. The man lost his balance and his gun and stumbled out into the street. Meeker, not knowing what was going on, moved out of the man's way.

"Stop him!" Deavers shouted. "He just robbed the bank."

Meeker turned and looked at the man in the street, who had fallen to his knees. On one side of him was his gun, and on the other side was the sack of money he had taken from the bank.

"Stop him! Stop him!" Deavers was shouting.

Meeker watched the robber, and when the man started to reach to one side the rancher drew his gun and fired. His shot struck the bank robber in the chest, and the man fell over onto the sack of money he had been reaching toward. His blood quickly stained the sack red.

Meeker stared down at the dead man, and then turned to look at Deavers as the man came running out of the bank. The bank manager immediately went to the body, rolled it off the sack of money, and picked the sack up. Cradling it, unmindful of the blood he was getting on his clothes, he stepped back up onto the boardwalk.

"Mr. Meeker," he said, "you just saved the bank a lot of money, sir."

"I did?" Meeker said. It still hadn't dawned on him what had happened. Still decidedly drunk, he stared down at the gun in his hand and shook his head.

"You're a hero," Deavers said.

"I am?"

"My friend," Harmon Deavers said, "the bank is going to give you that loan you need so desperately. Yes, sir, you're a bona fide hero."

Meeker looked at Deavers and said, "I'm a what?"

"A hero, man," Deavers said, clapping the man on the back, "the town hero!"

Chapter Fifteen

Clint and the sheriff, Del Hays, arrived on the scene at the same time. By then a crowd had gathered, and Deavers was telling them how brave Jack Meeker had been, tangling with the bank robber single-handedly and besting the man fair and square in a gun battle. From the way the bank manager was talking, one would think that the two men had emptied their guns at each other several times over, while Clint could only recall hearing one shot.

"Sheriff, Sheriff," Deavers said, spotting the man with the badge, "Mr. Meeker here just stopped a bank robbery and killed the robber."

"He did, huh?" Hays asked.

Clint looked at Meeker and found the man looking a bit befuddled.

Hays walked over to the bank robber, leaned over, and examined the man.

"Well, I'll be—" he said.

"What is it?" Clint asked.

Hays straightened up and pointed down at the dead man, looking around at the crowd.

"Do you know who this is?"

No one did.

"It's Shorty Bagwell."

"Shorty?" Clint asked.

"That's right."

"Who is he?" Clint asked.

"He's wanted for bank robbery all over the state," Hays said. "Hell, there's a five-hundred-dollar reward on his head."

Jack Meeker looked up and said, "Five hundred dollars?"

"Well," Deavers said, sounding happier still, "it sounds like you won't be needing that loan after all—although it's still there, if you want it."

Clint noticed that Meeker still had his gun in his hand. He could not remember his friend ever having killed anyone before.

"Jack," he said, moving next to the man, "holster your gun."

"Huh? What?" Meeker asked. He looked at Clint, his eyes still somewhat unfocused. If he was a hero, he was a very unlikely one.

"Put your gun away," Clint told him.

"Oh, yeah, sure," Meeker said, holstering the weapon.

"Sheriff," Deavers said, "I want you to make damn sure that Mr. Meeker here gets the reward."

"He'll get it, all right," Hays said. "I'll see to that."

"Fine, fine," Deavers said. "Mr. Meeker, after that, if you still want that loan you come and see me. This bank—hell, the whole town—owes you a debt."

The crowd started cheering, and Meeker started looking even more confused.

"Sheriff," Clint said, "do you need him for anything?"

"Not right now," Hays said. "I want to get this body off the street, and then I'll have to send a telegram about the reward money."

"Have them wire it to the bank," Deavers said. "That will give me the honor of handing the money to Mr. Meeker myself."

"All right," Hays said, "but it'll take a couple of days."

"We'll be back tomorrow," Clint said to Hays. "I want to get Jack home, right now."

"Sure," Hays said, "go ahead. Like I said, I don't need him."

"Come on, Jack," Clint said. "It's time to go home."

Amid loud cheering Clint and Jack walked to their horses, mounted up, and rode out of town.

As soon as they were alone Meeker looked at Clint and asked, "What the hell happened?"

"I'll tell you all about it," Clint said, "when we get you home."

"Shit," Meeker said, suddenly, "I don't feel so good." With that the hero leaned over and promptly threw up.

Chapter Sixteen

"He what?"

"Apparently," Clint said, almost helplessly, "he walked in on a bank robbery, killed the bank robber, and saved the money."

"Clint," Carol Meeker said, "Jack's no gunman."

"Well, the bank manager—a new one named Deavers—is telling the whole town what a hero Jack is."

"And what did Jack say?"

"You saw him," Clint said. She had just returned from putting the town hero to bed. "He's still not sure what happened, himself."

"What happened with the loan?"

Clint told her how Meeker had been turned down for the loan, and how he and Meeker had been drinking in the saloon when Clint asked if he had offered to borrow money against the value of the ranch.

"That's when he marched back to the bank and walked in on the robbery."

"He could have been killed!"

"But he wasn't," Clint said, "and now he's the town hero, and Deavers wants to give him the loan . . . *and* he's got a five-hundred-dollar reward coming to him."

"Five hundred dollars?" she asked, shocked.

"That's right."

"But that'll save us!"

"Well, at least something good will come out of this, then," Clint said, "but Jack still has to deal with the fact that the town sees him as a hero because he killed a man."

"Jack's never killed anyone before," she said.

"I know," Clint said. "That's what worries me."

He found out later that he was worrying for the wrong reasons.

It was a few hours later when Jack Meeker came out of the house while Clint was sitting on the porch.

"Hey," Clint said.

"Clint."

"How are you feeling?"

Meeker considered the question, then took a deep breath and said, "Good, I feel good."

"Do you?"

"Yeah," Meeker said, still considering the question. Then he nodded shortly and said, "Yeah, I feel damn good."

"Do you remember what happened?"

"Sure I do," Meeker said. "I stopped a bank robbery, and I got a five-hundred-dollar reward comin' to me."

"You killed a man, Jack," Clint reminded him.

"I know that," Meeker said, looking at Clint, "but he was a bank robber, right? He was wanted, and he had a gun. Hell, he could have killed *me*."

"That's true."

"Then that's that," Meeker said.

"He's the first man you ever killed, Jack."

"I know that, Clint," Meeker said. "Stop trying to make me feel guilty about it. I don't. I feel good. We're gettin' five hundred dollars, and I'm the town hero."

"Jack," Clint said, "about this hero stuff—"

"Don't worry, Clint," Meeker said, stepping down off the porch, "I can handle it. I'm just gonna take a little walk before dinner. See you later."

As Meeker walked away Clint could see that there was no trace of the slump the man had been walking with since his arrival, and probably for a long time before that. Jack Meeker's back was straight, his shoulders were squared, and he was walking tall.

Too bad it was all for the wrong reasons.

Jack Meeker ate with a hearty appetite that night, taking seconds and thirds.

"Eat up," he told Clint. "We got some money coming. When we get it we'll stock up on supplies.

We'll be eating high on the hog, won't we, honey?"

From behind him his wife looked at Clint Adams and said, "If you say so, Jack."

"Hell, sure I say so," Meeker said. "And we'll get this place back into shape, too. I mean, five *hundred* dollars. I never expected to get *that* when we went into town this morning."

"No," Carol said, "neither did I."

After dinner Meeker went out on the porch, sat down, and started cleaning his gun. Clint came out and saw him doing it, and doing it awkwardly.

"What are you doing that for?"

Meeker looked up and said, "Hey, a man's got to keep his weapon clean, right? You never know when you're going to use it."

"Jack," Clint said, "when's the last time you used your gun, before today?"

"I don't know," Meeker said, shrugging. "A long time ago, I guess."

"And never on another man, right?"

Meeker stopped what he was doing and said, "Why do you keep harpin' on that? Hey, look, somethin' happened today that I didn't go lookin' for, and a man got killed. But . . . damn it, I feel good about myself for the first time in a long time. Is there anythin' wrong with that?"

"No," Clint said, "no, Jack, there's nothing wrong with feeling good about yourself."

"Damn right," Meeker said. "Look, I'm gonna turn in. I want to get to town nice and early tomorrow and find out about my reward."

"Sure, Jack."

Meeker stood up, said, "Good night," and went inside.

Clint stayed out on the porch for a while and decided to head back to Texas the next day. He wasn't needed here anymore.

Chapter Seventeen

Clint rode into Little Rock with Jack Meeker the next morning. His intention was to stay one more night in the hotel, and then leave town the next day and head back to Texas.

Clint was surprised at the reception Jack Meeker got as they rode down the main street. People came out into the middle of the street to greet him and shake his hand. If Meeker was surprised, he didn't show it. He seemed to be accepting it as his due.

To Clint it seemed that his friend was taking this whole hero business much too much to heart.

They separated at the livery, Clint once again going to the hotel to check in.

"Mr. Adams," the desk clerk said, greeting him with forced graciousness, "so glad to have you back, sir. Would you care to have the same room?"

"Any room is fine," Clint said. The man was annoying him. He finished signing in and then said, "Would you have my belongings taken up to my room, please?"

"Of course, sir," the clerk said. "That will be the same room you had before."

"Fine, fine," Clint said.

He left the hotel and walked over to the sheriff's office. Meeker's planned first stop was to be the bank. On the way in he had told Clint that he was going to take advantage of the bank's willingness—the willingness of Harmon Deavers—to give him a loan now.

"Why not?" he'd said. "If they want to give me some money, let them. After all, I earned it."

Clint didn't say anything. He didn't feel that killing a man "earned" you anything. He knew plenty of bounty hunters, indeed had some who were his friends, but that didn't mean he approved of the way they made their living. Hunting a man—and killing him, if it came to that—was not something he felt one should be rewarded for. It should be left up to the lawmen, who were paid a salary for that sort of thing.

Clint entered the sheriff's office and was happy to see that Meeker wasn't there. He was probably still over at the bank.

Sheriff Del Hays looked up from his desk and said, "Mornin', Adams."

"Good morning, Sheriff."

"Somethin' I can do for you?"

"I'll be leaving town tomorrow morning."

"Well," Hays said, "thanks so much for comin' over to tell me that."

"That's not what I came to say," Clint said. "I'm worried about Jack Meeker."

"Meeker?" Sheriff Hays frowned. "What is there to worry about? The man is about to become five hundred dollars richer."

"That part is fine," Clint said. "It's what else might happen to him that I'm concerned about."

"I don't understand. What are you worried might happen?" Hays asked.

"The town is making him out to be some kind of hero," Clint said.

"Well, after all, he did save the bank's money," the sheriff said, "and that means he saved the money of a lot of people in town—including a lot of the town's most important people."

"Yes, but he did it—look, I'm not saying he doesn't deserve the town's thanks, but my God, man, what he did was practically an accident."

"So?"

"What do you mean, so?" Clint said. "Jack could take all of this hero stuff to heart, Sheriff."

"And what's wrong with that?"

"He might try to do it again," Clint said, "and next time maybe it will be someone more formidable than . . . Shorty Bagwell."

"Hey," Hays said, "Bagwell held up a lot of banks, Adams. He was no witless, accidental bank robber."

"Sheriff," Clint said, starting to feel helpless,

"I'm not trying to belittle anyone, I'm just trying to make sure that Jack Meeker doesn't start thinking he's some kind of gunman. Before yesterday, I don't think he had ever even fired his gun at a man before, let alone killed one."

"Adams," Hays said, "don't you think you should let your friend enjoy his moment in the sun? I mean, I understand he's had some hard times lately. Thanks to what happened yesterday, maybe those hard times are over, and what's wrong with that?"

"Nothing, but—"

"He'll be a hero for a while—a few days, maybe a few weeks—and then everythin' will get back to normal. Believe me, I'm not going to let anyone in my town start actin' like a vigilante. I'm still the law here, even though I wasn't the one who stopped the bank robbery yesterday."

Clint studied the man for a few moments and then said, "Maybe you're right. Maybe I am worrying for no good reason."

"I think you are," Hays said, "but I can't blame you for wantin' to look out for your friend. I tell you what. I'll keep my eye on him over the next few weeks."

"I'd appreciate it, Sheriff."

"You may not think much of me as a sheriff, Adams," Hays said, "but I care what happens in Little Rock."

"I'm sure you do, Sheriff," Clint said. "I'm sorry if we got off on the wrong foot."

"No problem," Hays said.

The lawman extended his hand, and Clint took it and shook it.

"Where will you be spending the day?" Hays asked.

"I'm back in the hotel, just overnight."

"Try and stay out of trouble, all right?"

Clint grinned and said, "You mean stay out of Ken Becker's way, don't you?"

Hays waved a hand and said, "I don't want to get into that again. Just take care, all right?"

"All right, Sheriff," Clint said. "You'll get no grief from me."

"Good."

"Uh, when will Jack's reward be available?"

"He'll be gettin' it today."

Clint frowned. "So quickly?"

"Mr. Deavers has decided to advance it to him," Hays said. "He's probably givin' it to him right now."

"Does anyone else in town know about that?"

"I don't think so," Hays said. "At least, I didn't tell anyone. I don't know about Deavers, though. Hell, he might have even told the editor of the newspaper, the *Little Rock Gazette.*"

"Jesus," Clint said, "I hope not. That'd make a target out of Jack Meeker for sure."

Hays rubbed his jaw and said, "You might have a point there. Why don't I take a walk over to the bank?"

"I'll tag along, if you don't mind."

"Why not?" Hays said, picking up his hat. "At least I can keep an eye on you, that way."

Chapter Eighteen

As Clint and the sheriff reached the bank, they saw that there was a small crowd gathered in front. When they got closer they could hear the voice of Harmon Deavers.

" . . . so the Little Rock Bank is proud to present Mr. Jack Meeker with his five-hundred-dollar reward for apprehending the notorious bank robber, Edward 'Shorty' Bagwell."

"Edward?" Clint said.

"Shorty's Christian name," Hays explained. "See that fella there?"

"I see him."

"That's Sam Florian, the publisher of the *Gazette*. It looks like Mr. Deavers is making a circus out of this whole thing."

"Is that worry I hear in your voice, Sheriff?" Clint asked. "What's there to worry about?"

Hays frowned, but didn't respond.

Deavers was continuing.

"In addition," the banker said in a fine example of theatrical oratory, "the bank is pleased to present Mr. Meeker with an additional two hundred and fifty dollars, to show its appreciation for his heroic actions."

"Heroic actions," Clint said, shaking his head.

"I don't like this," Hays said. "When this hits the newspaper, it could get picked up by other newspapers."

"And that could bring some trouble to town, right?" Clint said.

"Bank robbers are an odd lot," Hays said. "They actually take pride in what they do. Shorty might have had some friends who won't like what happened to him."

"And then all of this will become your problem, right?" Clint asked.

"Yeah," Hays said, "right."

As the crowd began to disperse, Hays said, "I think I'll go over and have a talk with Florian."

"Good luck," Clint said.

Hays looked at Clint and said, "Maybe you ought to have a talk with your friend."

"Believe me, Sheriff," Clint said, "I've *been* talking to him."

As Hays walked over to the newspaper publisher and editor, Clint decided instead to have a talk with Harmon Deavers. He waited while Deavers gave Meeker a hearty handshake and a slap on the back, and then Meeker turned and walked away. As Deavers went back into the bank,

Clint mounted the boardwalk and followed.

"Mr. Deavers."

The bank manager turned and stared at Clint. "Yes?"

"Can I talk to you for a minute?"

"Is this about bank business?"

Clint hesitated a moment, then said, "Yes."

Deavers looked around—for what Clint didn't know—and then said, "Very well, come into my office."

Deavers headed for his office and didn't seem to care whether Clint followed or not.

Once inside the room he moved around behind his desk, then looked at Clint as if surprised to see that he was still there.

"Yes?"

"Mr. Deavers, I'm a friend of Jack Meeker."

Deavers studied him for a few seconds, then something seemed to dawn on him.

"You're Mr. Adams, aren't you?"

"That's right."

"Well . . . what can I do for you, Mr. Adams?"

"I'd like you to stop trying to make a legend out of Jack Meeker."

"Mr. Meeker did this bank a great service, Mr. Adams," Deavers said. "I'm just trying to show my appreciation, and the appreciation of my depositors."

"You're going to get him killed, Mr. Deavers."

Deavers frowned and said, "I don't quite follow your reasoning."

"By making sure this all got in the newspapers

you've made Jack Meeker a target for any friends Shorty Bagwell might have had. By handing him all that money in front of the bank, you made him a target for any cheat or holdup man who might want to follow him home later and take it away from him."

"I'm sure Mr. Meeker can take care of himself," Deavers said. "After all, he did kill a bank robber yesterday, didn't he?"

"Sure," Clint said, "by accident."

Deavers gave Clint a look of disbelief and said, "How do you kill someone by accident, Mr. Adams? It seems to me that would be a fairly cold and deliberate act . . . one that you yourself are quite familiar with, if I understand correctly."

Clint decided to let the remark pass.

"Jack Meeker found himself at the wrong place at the wrong time, Mr. Deavers, and was fortunate enough to come out of the situation alive. He may not survive the next time."

"That's hardly something for me to concern myself about, Mr. Adams," Deavers said. "Mr. Meeker is a grown man, perfectly able to take responsibility for what he does with his own life."

"I see," Clint said. "You don't care what happens to Jack Meeker now?"

"My concern is for the bank and its depositors," Deavers said, squaring his chin and straightening his back. "It is what makes me so very good at my job, sir."

"And the publicity you can count on getting from

what happened yesterday?" Clint asked. "That doesn't worry you, at all?"

"It may attract more depositors, yes," Deavers said thoughtfully, as if he hadn't been thinking of that all along. "Is there anything wrong with that?"

"No," Clint said, "nothing wrong with it, but think about this, Mr. Deavers . . ." Clint paused, holding it until he saw Deavers actually lean forward in his seat. "When word gets out that Jack Meeker—a rancher—had to save your money for you—and your depositors—or a bank robber—one lone bank robber—would have gotten away with it, that might not attract depositors. In fact, it might even cost you some."

Clint turned, but not before he saw with some satisfaction that Harmon Deavers's jaw had dropped as he realized the truth of what Clint had said.

Chapter Nineteen

Clint was walking away from the bank, not sure where he was headed, when he saw Meeker coming at him.

"Clint, I been looking for you," Meeker said. "Did you hear—"

"I heard," Clint said, "and I saw, Jack."

"Well, come on, I'll buy you a drink," Meeker said.

"It isn't noon yet, Jack."

"Well, I feel like celebratin'," Meeker said, "and the Silver Bullet's open. Let's go."

Clint sighed, and then followed his friend to Ken Becker's Silver Bullet.

When they were seated at a back table with a beer each, Clint asked, "What happened with the loan?"

"I didn't need to ask for it," Meeker said, "not with the five hundred dollars that was on

Bagwell's head, and the extra two hundred and fifty that Mr. Deavers kicked in from the bank. I've got what I need now, Clint."

"Money, you mean," Clint said.

"Well, yeah, sure I mean money," Meeker said. "Jeez, I tell you, going back to that bank yesterday was the best thing that ever happened to me. I feel like a new man, Clint." He stared across the table at Clint and asked, "Is this what it's felt like for you all these years?"

"What do you mean?" Clint asked. He thought he knew what Meeker meant, but he was hoping that he was interpreting it wrong.

"I mean all those years of killing men," Meeker said. "Does it always feel this good?"

"Jesus, Jack . . ." Clint said, closing his eyes.

"What?"

Clint opened his eyes and tried to control his anger and his frustration.

"It doesn't feel *good* to kill a man, Jack. I mean, it's not *supposed* to."

"Not even when there's five hundred dollars involved?" Meeker asked.

"Killing is not a good thing, Jack," Clint said. "Come on, we teach *children* that."

"What about you?"

"What about me?" Clint asked.

"Your reputation—"

"You're talking like a horse's ass now, Jack," Clint said angrily. "How many years have you known me? Ten? Twelve?"

"Sure," Meeker said, "but you were the Gunsmith even before that. I mean, that reputation had to come from someplace, right?"

"Yeah," Clint said, "the fertile imaginations of newspapermen, like the one who's going to write about you tomorrow."

"Yeah, ain't that somethin'?" Meeker asked. "I'm gonna be in the newspapers."

"Jack," Clint said, "you better wake up to what's happening here. Once that story appears, you're going to be fair game for every cheap gunman who fancies himself a bank robber."

"Let 'em come," Meeker said. "Maybe they'll have prices on their heads, too."

Clint couldn't believe that the drivel he was hearing was coming out of the mouth of a grown man.

"Jack, you sound like a fifteen-year-old with his first gun."

Meeker stared across the table at Clint and said, "What's the matter, Clint? You don't want to share the fame?"

"What?"

"Sure," Meeker said, "people been writin' about you and hearin' about you for years. Now maybe they're gonna start hearin' about me, and you don't like it, huh?"

"Jack," Clint said, coldly, "think about what you're saying."

"I know what I'm sayin'," Meeker said. "My life's about to change, Clint, and if you don't like it, you don't have to be around to see it."

"Oh, I won't," Clint said, standing up. "I'll be

leaving in the morning, Jack."

"Well, say good-bye now, then," Meeker said.

Clint left his beer untouched.

"Thanks for the drink," he said. "Say good-bye to Carol for me."

Clint walked out of the saloon wondering if he should have had more patience with Jack Meeker, but maybe Harmon Deavers was right about one thing. A man should take responsibility for his own actions, and Jack Meeker was going to learn that, sooner or later.

Chapter Twenty

Clint was back in Labyrinth, Texas, a week when the first letter from Carol Meeker arrived. He was sitting in Rick's Place with the owner, his friend Rick Hartman, having breakfast when the letter was hand delivered to him.

He opened it, read it, and then tossed it on the table.

"Bad news?" Rick asked.

"No," Clint said, "it's a letter of apology."

"From Jack Meeker?"

Clint shook his head.

"His wife."

"What did she have to say?"

"Just that she heard the way Jack and I parted, and she wanted to apologize for the things he said."

"He told her what he said?"

"She's a smart woman," Clint said. "I'm sure

she can figure out what happened."

"Did she mention anything about him? I mean, about his, uh, attitude?"

"No," Clint said. "She just said she wanted to apologize."

"It's too bad about Meeker," Rick said. "It's never any fun losing a friend."

"No," Clint said, frowning, "it isn't."

Hartman looked across the table at Clint and could read his friend's mind.

"Hey, it wasn't your fault," he said. "None of it was your fault."

Clint looked startled for a moment, and then smiled across the table at Rick.

"I was just thinking . . ."

"Yeah, I know," Rick said, "you were thinking that maybe there was more you could have done, only there wasn't. Come on, Clint, Jack Meeker's a grown man, responsible for his own actions."

"So I've been told," Clint said.

"Well, whoever told you knows what they're talking about."

"It was a banker."

"Oh," Rick said. "Well, that *one* time he knew what he was talking about."

"Yeah," Clint said, "maybe. . . ."

Chapter Twenty-One

The second letter arrived a full six months later, only Clint wasn't in Labyrinth then. He was in San Francisco for a big poker game, and then after that he got into some trouble helping a friend in Sacramento. On the way back he stopped in Chicago and got into some trouble with the law because he was trying to help another friend. When he got that all cleared up he headed back to Labyrinth for a rest. Rick Hartman had taken the letter and put it with the rest of Clint's mail. It wasn't until four months after the letter's arrival that Clint returned to Labyrinth and read the letter.

He was in Rick's Place that night, nursing a beer at the bar when Rick approached him.

"I couldn't help noticing a letter from Little Rock waiting for you when you got back," he said. "Mind if I ask if it was from Meeker?"

"Carol Meeker."

"Another apology?"

"No," Clint said, frowning, "a plea for help."

"Uh-oh," Rick said. "What did she say was wrong?"

"She didn't say," Clint said. "She just said that she needed my help."

"Sounds like the lady knows how to pull the right strings," Rick said.

"What's that mean?"

"You tell me," Rick said. "You just got back from Sacramento and Chicago, where you got into trouble trying to help your friends. All a friend has to do, Clint, is *ask* you for help, and you're there—and if that friend happens to be a woman—"

"Okay, okay," Clint said, "I get your drift."

They stood there at the bar in silence for a few moments, and then Rick asked, "When are you heading back to Little Rock?"

Clint sighed and said, "In the morning."

"Well, good luck," Rick said.

"I'm probably going to need it."

Rick put his hand on Clint's arm and said, "You're a good friend, Clint."

"I wonder," Clint said, "what it's like to have no friends."

"No," Rick said, "you don't. . . ."

Chapter Twenty-Two

By the time Clint got back to Little Rock it had been almost a full year since his last visit. During that time the town had grown even more. Riding down the street Clint noticed that all of the buildings were now in use, and there were no more under construction. He wondered if Little Rock had reached its peak, if this was what the town would be like from now on, or if there was room for even more growth.

He left Duke at the livery and went to the same hotel where he had stayed the last time. One thing hadn't changed. The same desk clerk was there, and when he saw Clint enter the lobby a look of dread spread over his face, which transformed quickly into a wide, false smile.

"Mr. Adams," the clerk said, "back with us again, sir?"

"For a few days, maybe," Clint said.

"You're in luck, sir," the man said. "I can give you the same room."

Clint wanted to ask the man what he thought was so great about that room, but decided against it.

"That'll be fine."

"Would you like me to have someone take your things up?" the man offered.

"Please," Clint said, signing the register. "I'd appreciate it."

"Certainly, sir," the clerk said. "No problem."

"Thanks."

Clint left the hotel and walked over to the sheriff's office. If something was wrong—*really* wrong—maybe the lawman would know about it.

He entered the office and saw Del Hays sitting at his desk, going through wanted posters.

"Looking for anyone in particular?" he asked, closing the door behind him.

The man looked up and recognized Clint immediately.

"Adams," he said, "back again so soon?" He said it as if only a few days had passed since they had last seen each other.

"I happened to be in the neighborhood. . . ."

"Sure," Hays said. He stacked the posters neatly and set them aside. "Just passing the time seeing who's wanted for what. Uh, what brings you back this way?"

"I was hoping you could tell me that."

Hays frowned and said, "I don't follow."

"I got a letter from Carol Meeker telling me she needed my help," Clint said.

"I guess she would," Hays said. "It's kind of hard for a woman to run a ranch alone."

"Alone?" Clint asked. "What do you mean? Did Jack—"

"No, he didn't get himself killed," Hays said, "not that he hasn't been tryin'."

"Should I sit down for this?" Clint asked. "Is it going to take a while?"

"Have a seat, and I'll get you a cup of coffee," Hays said.

When they both had coffee Hays started his story.

"Not long after you left, a man came to town looking for Meeker," Hays said. "It was after the newspaper story appeared."

"Who was the man?"

"Nobody," Hays said, "a small-time drifter looking to make a name for himself."

"What happened?"

"Meeker killed him, slicker than spit."

"What?"

"You heard me right," Hays said. "The fella called Meeker out, and your friend killed him, fair and square."

"Jesus," Clint said, "I can imagine how Jack reacted to that."

"Oh, yeah," Hays said. "He thought he was the second comin' of Wild Bill, that's for sure. Started struttin' around town, hitchin' up his guns—"

"Guns?"

"That's right," Hays said. "He started wearin' *two* of 'em."

Clint closed his eyes and waved at Hays to continue.

"Pretty soon he was in town every day and never out at the ranch."

"What happened to the money he got for killing Bagwell?" Clint asked.

"Oh, he put that into the ranch, all right, got it up and runnin' again," Hays said, "and that was when he started hangin' around town. Miz Meeker's been tryin' to run that ranch alone for a while now."

"And Jack? Is he in town?"

"Uh, no, he ain't."

"He's out at the ranch?"

"Uh, no."

"Where is he, Sheriff?"

"He's huntin'."

"He's what?"

"He's bounty huntin'."

"What?"

"That's right," Hays said. "He started goin' out after bounty about—oh, five months ago."

The letter asking for help had arrived in Labyrinth about four months ago.

"See, he wasn't gettin' any takers in town," Hays said, "so he went out lookin' for them."

"Has he brought anyone in?"

"Oh, sure," Hays said. "I don't believe it either, Adams, but he's gotten good at it."

"I can't believe this. . . ."

"That ain't all," Hays said. "He's brought in about six men, and none of them alive." Hays stared at Clint and said, "You got yourself a real killer for a friend now, Adams."

"Jesus," Clint said. "Poor Carol. What she must be going through."

"Well, I don't know what she's going through, because she never comes to town," Hays said. "I think she's ashamed to."

"She would be," Clint said, standing up. "Knowing Carol, she would be. I better get right out there."

"He's really crossed the line, Adams," Hays said. "I ain't never seen anybody change that much, that fast, and it all goes back to Shorty Bagwell."

"I should have done something," Clint said, "*something* else while I was here."

"Hell, what could you have done?" Hays said. "He's a grown man, right?"

"Right," Clint said, "a grown man."

"I'm sorry, Adams," Hays said. "I know I said I'd watch out for him, but he hasn't done anything against the law. I mean, I don't *like* bounty hunters, but I can't arrest him for doin' it."

"I know, Sheriff," Clint said.

"Maybe you can do something now that you're here," Hays said, "talk to him, or somethin'. But to tell you the truth, I think he's too far gone. He's got a taste for it. He just flat-out *likes* it too much."

"Thanks for the information, Sheriff."

"Sure."

Clint was moving toward the door when Hays said, "Uh, where would you be plannin' on doin' your drinkin' while you're here?"

"Sheriff," Clint said, "I'm just not in the mood to be tiptoeing around anybody while I'm here."

"I know it," Hays said. "Just don't be lookin' for trouble, all right? One troublemaker in town at a time is plenty; I got enough to do tryin' to keep Meeker from shootin' some drunk for bumpin' into him."

"Yeah . . ." Clint said, depressed.

"Oh, another thing," Hays said.

"Now what?"

"Meeker hangs out at the Silver Bullet," Hays said. "He and Becker have actually become friends. He, uh, lets Meeker use any girl he wants, uh, for free."

Clint looked at Hays, who simply shrugged helplessly.

Clint left the office, retrieved Duke from the livery, and rode out to see how all of this had changed Carol Meeker.

Chapter Twenty-Three

The ranch had changed drastically, but for the better. Everything had been repaired. There were horses in the corral; there were even a couple of ranch hands working the animals.

"Can I help ya?" one of the hands asked as Clint rode up. He was young, about twenty-five, and thick through the shoulders and chest, while narrow in the hips. He removed his hat to mop his brow, revealing a thick head of curly brown hair.

"I came by to see Mrs. Meeker," Clint said.

"You a friend of hers?" the man asked, eyeing him critically.

Clint looked him over as well then looked over at the other man, who had stopped working to watch them. He was older, the other man, his face weathered from years of working outside. He was tall, thin, his body probably hardened by work.

Neither of them wore a gun.

"A friend of hers, and of *Mr.* Meeker."

"Him?" the man said. "He never comes around here."

"Where is Mrs. Meeker, then?"

"She's in the house," the man said, jerking his thumb over his shoulder.

"Thanks."

Clint rode up to the house, dismounted, and turned to look at the men. They were both staring at him. Were they protective of Carol? Or just curious about him?

He stepped up onto the porch and knocked on the door.

"Is that you, Sam?" Carol's voice called. "I was just making—" She opened the door and stopped short when she saw Clint. For a moment her face was unreadable, and then suddenly she smiled.

"Clint!"

"I got your letter, Carol," he said. "A little late, but I got it."

"I'd given up," she said.

He saw her look past him at the two men, and then she reached out and took both his hands.

"Come in, come in," she said.

She closed the door behind him and told him to sit down while she got him coffee. He watched her as she bustled about the kitchen. She had lost more weight, and it had made her even more beautiful. The woman who had been buried behind all those extra pounds all those years had finally come out, and she was a sight to behold. He had to

remind himself that she was married to a friend—
that is, a man who used to be a friend.

She brought him a cup of coffee and a piece of
fresh apple pie. She sat across from him with a
cup of coffee for herself.

"Tell me about it, Carol," he said.

"About what?"

"The reason you wrote asking for my help."

"Oh, that," she said. "That was silly, Clint. I
was starting to think that the letter got lost, and
I was glad it had. I'm sorry I made you come all
the way here for nothing."

"What do you mean, nothing?" Clint asked.
"Sheriff Hays told me that Jack's bounty hunting
now. I don't call that nothing."

"That's right," she said, "and he's good at it. He
keeps bringing money in for the ranch."

"I see," Clint said. "He turns the money over to
you for the ranch?"

"That's right," she said. "You see, he doesn't do
it for the money."

"Why does he do it, Carol?"

She stared at him a moment and then she said,
"Why does *any* man do what he's doing?"

"I know a few men who do it because they need
the money," Clint said. "Because there's nothing
else they know how to do. And then there are
the ones who just plain *like* it. Which is Jack,
Carol?"

She remained silent for a few moments, and
then she said, "He likes it, Clint. What can I tell
you? He must like it. He's always away; he's *never*

home. . . ." For a moment she started to sound bitter, but she suddenly stopped, and then she smiled. "Anyway, the place is coming along fine, isn't it?"

"You're doing a good job, Carol."

"Oh, it's not me," she said. "I've got two good men working the place."

"Is one the 'Sam' you thought I was?"

"What?"

"When I knocked on the door you said 'Sam,'" he told her.

"Did I?" She flushed, then said, "Yes, Sam Roberts and Toby Peters. You saw them working outside."

"Were they working for you when you wrote me that letter?" he asked.

"No," she said, "at that time I was . . . very alone, and scared."

Sure, he thought, and because he hadn't responded quickly enough, she had taken matters into her own hands, and now she wasn't alone anymore—not if he was reading the signs right.

"Carol," Clint said, "the sheriff told me that Jack has changed, in a lot of ways."

"He's changed in every way, Clint," she said. "He spends all his time either in town, or out hunting for some poor man who made the mistake of having a price placed on his head."

"He doesn't come home?"

She bit her bottom lip and said, "No."

"And that doesn't bother you?"

"It did," she said, folding her hands on the table.

"It did for a long time, Clint. When I wrote you that letter, I was desperate, and alone, and I didn't know what to do, but I'm fine now."

Sure she was. He could tell that from the whiteness of her knuckles as she clasped her hands tightly.

"And not alone anymore."

"No," she said, "I have Sam . . . a-and Toby, and they take care of the ranch for me."

"Carol . . . are you and Jack still . . . married?" he asked.

"Of course we are," she said, "only you wouldn't know it from the way he—well, you already know he doesn't come home—f-for *anything*. Everything he needs he gets . . . somewhere else. So we live apart now."

"And that suits you?"

She bit her bottom lip again and said, "Well, it has to, doesn't it? I mean, I don't want to go back to the way I was, you know. I didn't like being that weak, whining woman I was for a long time. I don't want to be that person again, Clint."

He reached across the table and put his hand over her two, which were straining against each other so hard he thought she would snap a finger for sure.

"No," he said, "I can see that, Carol."

She stared at him for a few moments, and then he felt her hands relax beneath his.

"Will you stay a while, Clint?" she asked. "I mean, you did come all this way because of me. The least I can do is prepare a meal for you."

"I'll stay for dinner," he said, "but I have a room back in town."

"Good," she said, taking his hand in hers, "good, stay for dinner, then. I'll make something special."

"Everything you make is special, Carol," he assured her. "I'll just go out and take care of my horse, all right?"

"All right, Clint," she said. "I'll get dinner started."

"I won't be long," Clint said. "I just want to look the place over."

"Go ahead," she said. "You'll like what you see. It's never looked this good."

"No," he said, marveling again at how beautiful she had become, "I can see that. . . ."

What a fool Jack was, he thought.

Chapter Twenty-Four

Clint went outside and led Duke over to the barn. He saw from the corner of his eye that the young man, Sam, was watching him. He couldn't blame Carol, he supposed. Jack had left her alone to fend for herself, aside from giving her money. So what if she had found solace in the arms of a younger man?

He was unsaddling Duke when he heard someone enter the barn behind him. He waited, and eventually the ranch hand, Sam, came into view. Clint was reminded of that time in the Little Rock livery when Ken Becker's men had tried to warn him off.

"Can I help you?" Clint asked.

"You stayin'?"

"What do you mean, am I staying?"

The man shifted his weight and licked his lips. "I mean," he said again, "are you staying?"

"I'm staying for dinner, son," Clint said. "I was invited. Is that all right with you?"

"As long as you ain't stayin'," the younger man said again.

Clint dropped Duke's saddle and took two quick steps which put him face-to-face with the man.

"And if I was staying?" he asked.

The younger man took a step back before he could stop himself.

"Mister, I don't know when you was here last, but things have changed around here," Sam Roberts said.

"So I understand."

"She told you?"

"What she told me is none of your business, son," Clint said. "That lady has been a friend of mine for a long time. I sure as hell don't have to explain myself to you when it comes to her."

"Look, you better understand—"

Clint cut the man off by poking him in the chest with his forefinger . . . hard.

"Are you trying to give me some kind of warning, sonny?" Clint said. "Because if you are, I'm here to tell you I don't take kindly to warnings."

He saw the younger man's eyes drop to the gun on his hip.

"This gun bother you?" Clint asked. "I can take it off, you know."

"Look, mister," Sam said, "I was just—"

"Get out," Clint said, starting to turn away from the man.

"What?"

"I said get out!" he snapped. He turned back, put both hands on the man, and shoved him toward the door. The other man caught his balance, paused a moment, and then kept on going out the door.

Jesus, Clint thought, what the hell am I doing? Why was he getting so angry at the kid? He was only trying to make his claim clear. And what claim was that? On a married woman a dozen years older than he was? A woman Clint had known for that many years?

He shook his head and started brushing Duke down, his brush strokes getting harder and harder until the big gelding shifted beneath them.

"Sorry, big boy," Clint said, patting Duke on the neck. "No point taking my anger out on you, huh?"

He wondered if the young ranch hand had gone to get a gun. What would he do if the kid came back with one? Kill him? Because he was mad at Jack Meeker for screwing up the life he had with Carol? A life Clint Adams would probably have killed for?

All these thoughts about killing. Wasn't that what had started this whole mess in the first place?

Clint decided then and there he wasn't leaving Little Rock this time until he had set Jack Meeker straight.

Chapter Twenty-Five

When Clint came out of the livery Sam Roberts was nowhere in sight, but the other man, Toby Peters, was walking over from the corral. Was he about to get another warning? he wondered.

"Toby Peters," the man said, introducing himself as he approached.

Clint took the man's hand and shook it. Peters had the gnarled fingers of a man who had worked with horses his whole life.

"The kid come on strong?" he asked.

"He did."

"Don't pay him no mind," Peters said. "He's love struck, you know?"

"I figured that out."

"You been friends with Miz Meeker a long time?"

"A long time," Clint said.

"And Jack?"

107

"You know Jack?" Clint asked.

"Enough to know he's gone plumb loco this past year," Peters said, shaking his head.

"I was here, back when it all first started," Clint said.

"That business with Shorty Bagwell?"

Clint nodded.

Recognition dawned on the man, and he said, "You're Clint Adams, ain't ya?"

"That's right."

"Jesus," Peters said, "the kid'll shit stones when I tell him he braced the Gunsmith."

"No, he won't," Clint said. "He's too young."

"You're right," Peters said.

"He's not likely to come looking for me with a gun, is he?" Clint asked.

"Normally, I'd say no," Peters said, "but that Miz Meeker, she's got his head spinning—not that I got nothin' against her, you understand. I mean, Jack leavin' her on her own and all."

"I understand," Clint said. "I remember what it was like to be that young, and in love."

"With an older woman, right?" Peters said. "One as pretty as her? Yeah, I remember that, too. I'll try to keep him out of your hair."

"And I'll try to keep my temper," Clint said. "I'm just so mad at Jack—and at myself."

"Why yourself?"

"I just feel like I could have stopped this."

"How?"

"I don't know," Clint said. "Maybe I can think of a way now."

"I don't know," Peters said, shaking his head. "I seen the look in Jack's eyes, ya know? I seen it on other men plenty of times."

"And?"

"And they usually end up dead."

"Well," Clint said, "hopefully I can keep that from happening."

"You wanna get them back together?"

"That would be nice."

"A lot of water under the bridge," Peters said. "Jack's got hisself a taste of the wild life, runnin' with whores, hangin' around with Ken Becker—"

"You know Becker?" Clint asked.

"Enough to know he's a man to stay away from," Peters said. "He just keeps feedin' Jack's ego, ya know?"

"I know," Clint said. "Is Deavers still the bank manager?"

"Bank *president*," Peters said. "There's another good man to stay away from. You gonna be stayin' out here, or in town?"

"In town," Clint said. "I don't want to tempt the kid. I'll just be stayin' here for dinner."

"Well, like I said," Peters told him, "I'll try to keep the kid out of your hair while you're here."

"I appreciate it," Clint said.

"Hey," Peters said, "I'm just tryin' to keep the kid from gettin' hisself killed."

"You're a good friend."

"Hell," Peters said, "friendship ain't got nothin' to do with it. I just don't want to end up doin' all the work out here by myself is all."

Chapter Twenty-Six

Carol made a wonderful dinner but ate very little of it herself. She urged Clint to eat, and he did the meal justice by eating three helpings.

"I'll get you some coffee and another piece of pie," Carol said while she was cleaning off the table.

He didn't argue. She seemed genuinely pleased to have him there, and to be able to cook for him. He wondered if she cooked for Sam Roberts, or if he was just taking Jack's place in her bed.

When he had the pie and coffee in front of him he said, "Carol, sit with me so we can talk."

"About what?" she asked. "Jack?"

"Yes, about Jack."

"I don't want to talk about him, Clint."

"Carol, have you given up on him?"

"*I'm* not the one who's given up," she said. "He gave up on me—on us—a long time ago."

"Well, what happened after I left?"

Finally she sighed and sat down with him.

"He just changed, Clint. Oh, not all at once. First he was basking in all that hero stuff, but that started to wear off after a couple of months. He actually started to get crabby about it, that people *weren't* treating him like a hero anymore. That was when he finally started to do some work around the ranch. And then . . ."

"And then what?"

"And then that other man came to town, looking for him," she said. "Someone from town rode out here and said there was a bank robber in town, saying he was going to hold up the bank in Jack Meeker's town."

"How did Jack react to that?"

She laughed shortly, totally without humor.

"He jumped up and strapped on his gun, said he was going right into town," she said. "I begged him not to go, but he said that he'd been practicing with his gun and he was ready."

"Was he practicing?"

"Every day," she said. "He'd go out behind the barn and shoot at bottles, cans, small animals, anything. And he was practicing drawing his gun and firing."

"I guess he *was* ready."

"Yes," she said. "At first I was glad that he had killed the other man and not killed himself, but Clint . . . when he killed that other man, he also killed the Jack Meeker I knew and loved. He changed drastically after that. That's when he started staying in town all the time, and when he bought those new guns, with pearl handles. He'd hang around that Silver Bullet, and men would buy him drinks, and the women . . . well, he developed a taste for *those* women."

Clint wondered idly if Harry had been one of *those* women Jack had developed a taste for.

"Soon he wasn't coming home at all, and he was going out hunting for men with prices on their heads," she said. "That Mr. Becker from the saloon was encouraging him, telling him that the more men he killed, the bigger his reputation would get."

She fell silent, staring at the floor, then lifted her eyes to look at him. They were moist, and she wiped at them angrily.

"I swore I wouldn't cry anymore," she said, "not for him, not for *that* Jack Meeker. Whatever happens to him he deserves."

"He'll end up dead soon enough, Carol," Clint said. "Sooner or later he'll go after the wrong man, and he'll get killed."

"That will be . . . too bad," she said, "but I have to go on with my life, Clint."

"Does that include Sam Roberts, Carol?"

She glared at him then, her chin thrust forward.

"I was lonely, damn it," she said, "and Sam is . . . very attentive."

"And young."

"So he's young," she said. "What about all the women Jack has had over the past few months?

A lot of them have been young. Why shouldn't *I* have a young stud if I want one?"

"No reason, Carol," he said, "no reason at all . . . if that's what you want."

She stared at him for a few moments, then reached for his hand.

"Maybe . . . now that you're here . . . it's not what I want. . . ."

He slid his hand away from hers gently.

"Carol, don't—"

"Don't you find me attractive, Clint?" she asked, standing up.

"Carol . . . you're attractive, you know that . . . you're beautiful. . . ."

She unbuttoned her dress quickly, and before he could say anything she had pulled it down to her waist, exposing her breasts. They were firm, and large, with wide, brown nipples. The rest of her had grown slim, but her breasts were still full and firm.

"Clint . . ." she said, thickly. She dropped the dress to the floor and stepped out of it.

Her thighs, like her breasts, had maintained their roundness, and she turned to show him her full, firm buttocks.

"Carol . . ." he said, his mouth dry.

"The last time you were here," she said, "I saw you looking at me . . . wanting me. Don't deny it, Clint. You want me."

She came to him then, her tongue entering his mouth, her breasts pressing against him, her hands caressing him, and he *couldn't* deny it, and didn't want to. He lifted her in his arms and carried her into the next room. He put her down on the bed and quickly removed his own clothes. She reached for him, holding his manhood, pulling him onto the bed, and then lowering her mouth to him, taking him inside while her nails scratched his inner thighs and her fingers fondled his testicles. He was so swollen he thought he would explode, and then he did, into her mouth . . . and that was just the beginning. . . .

He turned her over and began to explore her body with his mouth. He sucked her nipples, bit them, kissed his way down over her belly and then nestled comfortably in her pubic thatch, his tongue eagerly lapping at her.

"My God," she said, breathlessly, "my God, what are you doing . . . nobody's ever done that . . . ohhh . . ."

She couldn't talk after that, she just moaned and cried out, holding his head tightly so that he couldn't get away. He slid his hands beneath her, cupping her firm ass, and lifted her off the bed so he could lick all of her. . . .

He lowered her to the bed a little while later and then mounted her, entering her swiftly, piercing her all the way to her core. She gasped and tightened her powerful thighs around him.

He drove himself into her again and again, completely forgetting that she was his friend's wife. Even if he had thought about it, hadn't she herself said that her husband was dead to her? And what of the Jack Meeker who had been his friend for so many years? Was he gone as well? Later, he would try to justify what he had done, but at the moment he wasn't thinking of anything but the woman beneath him, and how eager she was for him, and how good she felt, and smelled, and tasted. . . .

Later while she slept, he crept from the bed, dressed, and went into the other room. He cleaned off the table, washed the dishes, and then left the house to go back to town. He still had not begun trying to justify what he had done. That would come later.

It was dusk outside, and neither of the men— Roberts or Peters—were around. That suited him. He went to the stable, saddled Duke, and rode back to town. He wondered how long he would have to wait before Jack Meeker got back from his latest hunt.

Chapter Twenty-Seven

When Clint reached town he left Duke at the livery and walked over to the Silver Bullet. It was fairly obvious that when Meeker came back that's where Clint would find him.

It was during the ride back to town that he thought about what he had done with Carol— his friend's *wife*—and tried to reason it away by telling himself that, to both of them, the old Jack Meeker was gone. He couldn't quite accept that totally, though. At least, not until he saw Meeker for himself. No matter how much the man had changed, there had to be *some* part of the old Jack Meeker there, and if there was, then maybe he could reach him.

When he entered the Silver Bullet the night's festivities were just about in full swing. The gaming tables were open, and it soon became obvious that he had made it just in time for one of Danielle's performances.

He walked to the bar, found a space, and ordered a beer from Lenny.

"Hey . . ." Lenny said, pointing to him in recognition.

"Hello, Lenny."

"Mr. Adams, right? Sure. It's been a while since you been here, but I remember you."

"I'm flattered," Clint said. "Have you seen Jack Meeker around?"

"Jack?" Lenny said. "Not for about a week now. He's out, uh—hey, wait—"

"Don't worry, Lenny," Clint said, "I know all about it."

"Ya do, huh?" Lenny said, leaning on the bar. "Funny how some people's lives can change, huh?"

"Yeah," Clint said, "funny."

"I gotta go," Lenny said. "Busy night. Harry's around, though . . . somewhere."

"Thanks."

Lenny went to pour somebody else a beer, and Clint turned with his mug in his hand and looked around the room. He spotted Harry right away, although she didn't see him right away. It surprised him how much pleasure he got out of seeing her.

He kept surveying the room, but there was no sign of Jack Meeker or, for that matter, Ken Becker. He walked over to the poker table and noticed that the dealer was someone he didn't remember. Probably the replacement for the man who had been cheating.

"I owe you," a voice said from behind him.

He had sensed someone behind him, so he turned slowly and looked at Ken Becker.

"That dealer," Becker said, inclining his head toward the poker table, "you were right about him. He *was* cheating. I owe you for that."

"Glad I could help," Clint said.

"You looking for Harry?"

"I thought I might say hello, while I was here," Clint said.

"Uh-huh," Becker said. "And what brings you back to Little Rock?"

"I just thought I'd stop in and see how my old buddy Jack was doing."

"He's doing just fine," Becker said. "He's a big man now."

"Is that a fact?"

"He's getting himself a reputation."

"I wish I could say I was glad to hear that."

"Why? You think you're the only one who should have a reputation?"

"I didn't choose mine," Clint said.

"That sounds like a long story," Becker said. "You'll have to tell me about it sometime." His tone of voice made it clear that, as far as he was concerned, "sometime" was the same as "never."

"There'll be a free beer waiting for you at the bar," Becker said.

"Thanks," Clint said. "I'll take it."

"Sure," Becker said, "don't mention it. You might even want to play some poker. It'll help you kill time until Jack gets back."

"I might at that," Clint said.

"You *are* going to wait for Jack to come back, aren't you?"

"Sure," Clint said. "I've got something I want to talk to him about."

"Jack's not much of a talker these days," Becker said. "He's become more of a doer."

"I understand you've given him a lot of encouragement in that department."

"I just like having the guy around," Becker said. "Enjoy yourself, Adams. Danielle's coming on in a couple of minutes."

"I can't wait."

Becker looked at him for a moment, wondering if he was being sarcastic, and then nodded and walked away.

Clint was following Becker's progress with his eyes as the man made his way toward the stage, probably to introduce Danielle himself. Harry entered his line of vision, though, getting between him and Becker, and he had to admit it was a distinct improvement.

She smiled, obviously very happy to see him, and he smiled back, a genuine smile of affection and appreciation as she approached him.

Chapter Twenty-Eight

"Tell me you came all this way just to see me," Harry said to him.

"I came all this way just to see you."

"Liar," she said. "But I'm glad to see you, no matter what brought you back."

Clint had spent the last night in Little Rock with Harry and had left her asleep the next morning when he slipped out and left town.

"It was mean of you to leave while I was asleep," she said to him now.

"I didn't want to wake you," he said. "You were sleeping so soundly."

"I was tired," she said. "You know how to say good-bye to a girl."

"Thank you."

"Do you know how to say hello, too?" she asked, giving him a sly look.

"Maybe you'll find out," he said, "later."

"No maybe about it, friend," she said, poking him in the belly with her forefinger and twisting it. "I'll see you later."

She went back to work, and he returned to the bar to get his free beer from Lenny. At that moment Becker appeared on stage and introduced his "wife," Danielle.

"Wife?" Clint said to Lenny.

"I told you," Lenny said, "some things change."

Maybe that was why Becker had asked Clint if he had come to see Harry, and had asked the question as if he didn't care.

"When did that happen?" Clint asked Lenny as the music started up.

"About three months ago."

All conversation ceased then as Danielle started her song. If anything, she looked as if her bosom had gotten bigger during the past year, but still, she was far from fat. It also seemed as if she hadn't lost any of her energy. Maybe being married gave her even more.

The place went crazy while she sang and jiggled about and even crazier after she finished, but she did only one song and got off the stage. Now that she was the boss's wife, she probably got to do as many—or as few—songs as she wanted to.

"How'd she manage to get Becker to marry her?" Clint asked Lenny after the din had died.

"She put it to him flat out," he said. "Marry her or she was movin' on. He didn't want to lose her. She's too good for business."

"So how has *his* life changed since being married?" Clint asked.

Lenny smiled and said, "It ain't, much. Oh, if you're wonderin' about Harry, though, her and the boss have got an understanding."

"Really?"

"Yeah," Lenny said, "he understands that she don't fool around with no married men."

"That's a good understanding to have."

"Of course," Lenny added, "there's women who don't care about that."

"I'm sure there are."

"A couple of them in this room tonight," Lenny added with a leer.

Lenny went off to do some more pouring, and Clint decided he was either going to have to keep drinking beer while he was waiting for Meeker to show up, or do something more productive.

He wandered over to the poker table and watched the game long enough to decide that the dealer was dealing a fair game. The next chair that came up empty, he filled.

Chapter Twenty-Nine

Clint's luck at the poker table was good. It wasn't great, but he did pretty well and came away a winner after a few hours of play.

"Y'all come back," the dealer said to him when he cashed himself out.

"I might just do that," Clint said.

"Bring some of our money back with you," one of the other players said, but he said it good-naturedly.

"I'll do that."

He went back to the bar and ordered his third beer of the night.

"How'd you do?" Lenny asked.

"I got by."

Lenny shrugged and moved on down the bar.

Harry came up to him and asked him the same question, and he gave her the same answer.

"I hope you took some of Ken's money."

123

"I understand your boss is married now," he said, changing the subject.

"Afraid I'll want you to spend some of it on me, huh?" she asked. "Okay, change the subject. Yeah, the old cow finally roped him."

"And you and he came to an understanding."

"Yeah, I told him I didn't fool around with married men, and he stopped chasing me."

"Did he ever catch you?"

She gave him a look and said, "You're not the only one who can change the subject."

"Okay," he said. "Tell me about Jack Meeker."

"What about him?" she asked. "He's *your* friend."

"He's not the man I knew anymore," he said. "I understand he hangs around here a lot."

"That's right."

"I also understand he makes, uh, liberal use of the girls."

"That's right, too," she said, "and before you ask, no, I'm not one of the girls he makes liberal use of. Gee, I never heard it put that way before."

"I just don't know how to talk around women," he said.

"Stick around," she said. "I'll teach you how to communicate *without* talking."

"That sounds like something worth learning," he said.

"Give me another hour in this place," she said. "Ever since the boss stopped chasing me around his desk, I've got to give an honest day's work for an honest day's pay."

"The nerve of some people and what they expect of other people," he said, shaking his head.

She went back out onto the floor to do her job. At that moment the front door opened, and Sheriff Del Hays walked in. He paused just inside to look around, and when he saw Clint he walked over to him.

"I thought I might find you here," he said.

"Becker and I had a nice talk," Clint said. "I even played poker."

"I'm not worried about that," Hays said. "I just heard from the sheriff in Visalia."

Clint frowned.

"Where's that?"

"About fifty miles east," Hays said.

"What'd he have to say?"

"Seems Jack Meeker brought a man in there today, fella with a two-hundred-dollar bounty on his head."

"I see," Clint said, "and how did he bring this fella in?"

"How else?" Hays asked. "Slung over his own saddle."

Clint looked down at the beer in his hand, lost his taste for it, and set the mug down on the bar.

"Meeker'll be back tomorrow," Hays said. "I thought you might want to know."

"I appreciate it, Sheriff," Clint said.

"He'll stop in and see me first," Hays said. "He always does, and then he'll stop over here . . . for a girl, most likely."

"Is that a routine of his?"

"Yeah," Hays said. "He says there's somethin' about killin' a man that gives him the urge . . . if you know what I mean."

"I know what you mean," Clint said. "I've known men like that before . . . sick men." It made *him* sick to think that a man he had once called a friend had turned into a man like that.

"I'm sorry," Hays said, "I really am."

Clint nodded and studied the bar top. Hays turned and left the saloon without another word.

Clint looked up and waved Lenny over.

"Would you tell Harry I went back to my hotel?"

"Sure," Lenny said. "Want me to tell her to come over there?"

"That's up to her, Lenny," Clint said. "She'll know what to do."

"Okay," Lenny said with a shrug.

"Thanks."

Clint had to leave the saloon. He suddenly felt the need for some air, and the space to breathe it.

Chapter Thirty

Clint walked slowly to the hotel, breathing deeply to try to dispel the sick, queasy feeling in his stomach. Everything he had heard about Jack Meeker that day made the man out to be some kind of . . . monster. How could he have been friends with someone for twelve years and never—not once—seen that side of him? And what about Carol? How could she have been married to Meeker that long and never seen it? Did he hide it that well? Or was it simply that it was there the whole time, below the surface, waiting for the time when something would bring it out— something like the incident with Shorty Bagwell. Could the simple—or not-so-simple—act of killing a man have unleashed the monster in Jack Meeker?

Clint went up to his room, removed his gun belt and hung it on the bedpost, and sat slumped on the bed. Thinking about the monster in Jack Meeker started him thinking about the monster within him. Had he seen that monster, yet? Or was it still there, deep inside of him, waiting for something to awaken it? Was that monster in everyone? He preferred to think that it was not. It couldn't be. And yet if a decent man like Jack Meeker—like the Jack Meeker *he* knew—could be taken over . . .

He stood up and angrily paced the room. Sitting there crying about it, wondering about it, did no good. He was just becoming alternately depressed and angry. Now he wished he had stayed in the saloon, where he couldn't have this time alone to . . . mope.

At that moment, as if on cue, there was a knock at the door.

"Am I glad—" he started, thinking it was Harry, but it became immediately obvious that it was not as three shots ripped through the door, barely missing him. Whoever it was had been overanxious and had fired before Clint was in front of the door.

Clint fell back, leaped over the bed, grabbed his gun from his holster, and then ran for the door. He flattened himself against the wall, reached for the doorknob carefully, turned it, and swung the door open. Of course that took time, and by the time he stepped out into the hall the assailant was gone. Still, he felt he might as well go through the motions.

He ran down the stairs to the lobby, where his friendly clerk was gaping at him.

"Did you see anyone come through here?" he asked.

"I—I—I—" the man stammered.

Clint ignored him and ran out into the street. Outside, it was possible no one had heard the shots. It was dark, and the street was empty. He could hear the noise still coming from the Silver Bullet. He turned and went back inside. The clerk was still staring.

"Tell me what you saw," Clint said.

"I—I didn't see anyone come in," the clerk said nervously, "b-but I saw someone run out, a-after I heard the shots."

"Who was it?"

"I don't know."

"Would you know him if you saw him again?"

"I—I—it happened so fast," the man said helplessly. "I really didn't see his face."

"What *did* you see?"

"A figure," the man said. "He came running down the stairs, with a gun in his hand, and went out the front door. Th-that's all I saw."

"Was he short, tall, old, young? Come on, man! Give me something."

"Uh, young, I think," the clerk said, closing his eyes as if trying to see the man again, "from the way he moved. Uh, tall, big shoulders—"

"Curly brown hair?" Clint asked.

"He was wearing a hat," the clerk said. "But now that you mention it, I think he did have brown hair."

Sure, and if he asked if the man had a green

nose, the clerk would say, "Well, now that you mention it . . ." Clint decided now was the time to stop asking questions.

"All right," Clint said.

"Should I send for the sheriff?"

"No," Clint said, "there's no need to bother him now. Nothing else will happen tonight. I'll talk to him myself in the morning."

"Was there, uh, any damage?"

"To me, or the room?" Clint asked, then decided not to wait for an answer. "There are some holes in my door, but none in me."

"Do you, uh, want another room?"

"No," Clint said, "this one is fine. Don't worry about it. I'm not going to sue."

"Sue?" the clerk squeaked. "For what?"

"If I catch cold from the draft."

"Mr. Adams . . . . Mr. Adams!" the clerk called.

Clint went back upstairs without answering. He examined the holes in his door and was convinced that, had he been standing in front of it, he'd have at least two holes in him right now. Luckily, he'd been slow in answering the knock.

There was no doubt in his mind that the culprit was Sam Roberts. The young man obviously felt his relationship with Carol Meeker was threatened enough that he'd decided to commit murder. No one should be *that* much in love. He holstered his gun, not quite sure what he was going to do about this.

There was another knock on his door then, and he played it safe.

"Who is it?" he asked from where he was.

"Harry."

He walked to the door and opened it. Harry was staring at the holes in the door.

"I hope there aren't any of these holes in you," she said.

"No," Clint said, "luckily the shooter missed."

"It looks like he wanted you real bad," she said. She leaned over, put her finger in one of the holes, wiggled it around, and then withdrew it. "Who was it?"

"I have an idea," he said, backing up and allowing her to enter.

"Are you going to share it with me?"

"I will," Clint said, closing the door, "when it's a fact, and not an idea."

"You only got to town today, right?"

"That's right."

"Who did you get mad at you that quickly?"

"I don't know," Clint said. "Are you sure your boss isn't after you anymore?"

"In his dreams maybe," she said, removing her shawl, and then matter-of-factly removing her dress.

"Make yourself comfortable," he said.

Chapter Thirty-One

When Jack Meeker rode into town the next morning, Clint was sitting in a chair in front of the hotel. He sat forward as Meeker passed him, narrowing his eyes, not believing what he was seeing. Meeker had grown a beard and had allowed his hair to grow down to his shoulders. He looked for all the world like a poor man's Wild Bill Hickok. Now Clint knew why Hays had made the Wild Bill remark.

He watched as Meeker rode up to the sheriff's office and dismounted. To Clint the pearl-handled revolvers in the man's holsters looked ridiculous.

He sat back in his chair while Meeker took care of his business with the sheriff. His original plan had been to brave Meeker as soon as he rode in, but now he really didn't feel up to approaching him. Not with him looking the way he did. Jesus, if it wasn't so sad, he would have been laughing.

The fact of the matter was, in order for Meeker to have killed as many men as he had already killed, he *had* to have some ability with his gun. That had to have been another dormant quality of the man that had been awakened. Just how much ability he had with his gun, though, still remained to be seen. If he was hunting Shorty Bagwells, or men with two hundred dollars on their heads, then he had yet to be tested.

Maybe, Clint thought, maybe *he* was the man who should test him.

Another reason he didn't want to approach Meeker at that moment was his anger. This was new anger. Clint and Hickok had been very good friends, and it galled Clint that Meeker had chosen to try to look like Hickok, or otherwise pattern himself after the man. Hickok had been shot in the back and killed by a coward, and Clint did not like his memory being trod upon.

Clint decided not to wait for Meeker to come out of the sheriff's office. He got up and walked down the street to have lunch and to try to get himself in a proper frame of mind to deal with Jack Meeker.

"Clint Adams is in town," Sheriff Del Hays told Jack Meeker.

"Is that a fact?" Meeker said. "I wonder what he wants?"

"I guess he wants to talk to you."

"Well," Meeker said, "maybe I don't want to talk to him. Maybe if he knows what's good for him, he'll stay away from me."

"Meeker, look," Hays said, "I think your wife asked him for some help. There's no harm in—"

"My wife?" Meeker said. "Wait a minute. Was he out to see my wife?"

"Yeah, I think he went out there."

"Maybe that's why he came back, then," Meeker said, almost as if he were talking to himself.

"What do you mean?"

"He's after my wife."

Hays stared at Meeker with his mouth open.

"What the hell are you talking about?" the lawman asked. "You know, I knew you went crazy, but I didn't know *how* crazy."

Meeker stared coldly at Hays, who assumed that the look was supposed to frighten him.

"Sheriff," Meeker said, "it's only because you *are* the sheriff that I don't make you eat those words."

"Meeker," Hays said, "don't get carried away on me. You want to act tough, do it with some of your friends at the saloon. They *buy* this shit."

"Shit?"

"Yeah," Hays said, "the long hair, the mustache, the pearl-handled guns."

"Are you sayin' there's somethin' wrong with the way I look?" Meeker asked.

Helpessly, Hays said, "No, I'm not sayin' that at all, Meeker. Look, you got your reward. Adams is lookin' for you. Talk to him, that's my advice to you."

"Maybe you're right," Meeker said. "I'll *talk* to my old friend Clint." He turned and walked to the door, then turned back and added, "But maybe he won't like what I have to say."

After Meeker had gone Hays sat behind his desk, wondering what he should do about the man. He had obviously gone stark raving mad, and if Hays didn't do something, Meeker might actually hurt an innocent person.

Meeker stepped outside the sheriff's office and stood there, looking around. When you had a reputation like he did, there was always some cheap gunman lurking around the corner, waiting to try you out. He kept looking about until he was sure no one was watching him, then he hitched up his pearl-handled guns and walked his horse over to the livery. Clint Adams may have been looking for him, but let him look all he wanted. First, Jack Meeker had some urgent business to attend to at the Silver Bullet.

Chapter Thirty-Two

After lunch Clint went over to the sheriff's office. The sheriff was in, and for a moment he wondered if the man ever made rounds. Every time he went to the office, he found the man there, sitting behind his desk. That was probably unfair. After the first impression they had made on each other, Hays had turned out to be a fairly decent man. Of course, that didn't make him a good *law*man.

"Meeker's in," Hays said as Clint entered.

"I know," Clint said. "I saw him."

"Talk to him?"

"No," Clint said, taking a seat, "I *saw* him. I almost didn't recognize him."

"I told you," Hays said, "he thinks he's Hickok—and he's gettin' worse."

Hays told Clint about the man's attitude when

Hays told him that Clint was looking for him.

"I think he might be getting himself ready to try you," Hays said.

"I hope not."

"Be hell on you to have to kill a friend," Hays said.

"I've got to do something," Clint said, "if only for Carol's sake."

"How is she doin'?"

"Actually," Clint said, "she seems to be doing all right. She's got a couple of men working the ranch for her, and she seems to have resigned herself to being without Meeker."

"Might be the best thing for her," Hays said.

"Maybe," Clint said. "By the way, my hotel room door has three holes in it."

"How'd you manage that?"

"Not me," Clint said. "I was on the other side when the bullets came flying through."

"I'll assume you ain't hurt," Hays said. "What about the other man?"

"I never saw him," Clint said, "but the desk clerk did."

"Did he know him?"

"No," Clint said, "just said he was tall, and moving fast. He saw him going out, but not coming in."

"Maybe I'll go over and have a talk with him," Hays said. "It might jog his memory."

"I . . . might have an idea about who it was," Clint said, "but if you don't mind, I'd like to keep it to myself for a little while longer."

"You ain't thinkin' about settlin' this yourself, are you?" the sheriff asked.

"Not the way you think, no," Clint said. "I just think I can handle it."

"It's up to you," Hays said. "You're the one who was shot at. If you need any help, though, you let me know."

"I'll do that." Clint pushed himself up out of the chair.

"You gonna talk to Meeker now?"

"I might let him calm down some," Clint said.

"Yeah," Hays said, "it might be wise to wait until after he's had himself—uh, after he goes to the Silver Bullet. The mood he's in now, he just might want to try you with those pearl-handled guns of his."

Clint shook his head, once again recalling the sight of Meeker riding into town.

"Do you have a doctor in town?" Clint asked.

"Sure, Doc Platt," Hays said. "His office is above the hardware store, couple of streets down. Why?"

"Well, if I'm dealing with a sick man here," Clint said, "maybe the doctor can help me figure out a way *to* deal with him."

"Doesn't sound like a bad idea," Hays said. "Worth a try, anyway."

"Yeah," Clint said. "I'll see you later."

"Be careful," Hays said. "It sounds like you got more trouble to deal with than just Jack Meeker."

"I can handle it," Clint said.

"I hope so," Hays said. "It'll make my job easier if you do."

Chapter Thirty-Three

Clint found the doctor's office with no problem, and the doctor was there. The man asked Clint in and invited him to sit. He offered him a drink, which Clint refused.

"I hope you don't mind if I have one?"

"No, go ahead."

The doctor poured himself a short whiskey and tossed it down.

"What can I do for you?"

Clint told the man that he had a problem with an old friend, who seemed to have turned his back on the decent life he'd led for so long.

"Are we talking about Jack Meeker?" the doctor asked. "The hero of Little Rock?"

"You don't believe that, do you, Doc?" Clint asked. If the man did believe it, then he was talking to the wrong doctor.

"Of course I don't," the doctor said. "Making a

man a hero because he kills is asinine."

Dr. Anson Platt was in his sixties, white-haired and slim, with a ramrod straight back and the clearest blue eyes Clint had ever seen on a man.

"What's your connection to Meeker?" the man asked.

"We were friends until all of this started," Clint said.

"And what do you want from me?"

"I want to know if he's, uh . . ."

"Mad? Crazy? Insane?"

"Well . . . yes."

"There's no way to tell that," the doctor said. "No way for me to tell, anyway."

"What about if you examine him?"

"Insanity is an illness of the mind," the doctor said. "That's not my field. You'd have to have some specialist examine him."

"Well, can you at least give me an opinion?" Clint asked.

"Tell me everything," the doctor replied, "and then I'll see."

Clint told him about the Jack Meeker he'd known for almost a dozen years, and then what had happened to the same man since the incident in front of the Little Rock bank. He also explained what had become of the man's marriage to a woman Clint was sure he had once loved very much.

"Well," the doctor said, "it sounds like we're talking about a complete personality change."

"Does that mean he's crazy?"

"It means he's changed," the doctor said, "and not for the better."

"Doc," Clint said, "if he comes after me I'm going to have to defend myself."

"So what do you want from me?"

"I guess I want you to tell me that if I end up killing him, I won't be killing the man I knew for so long."

"*That's* crazy," Dr. Platt said. "Of course he's the same man; he's just not *acting* the same way."

Clint rubbed his hand over his face and let out a breath.

"Mr. Adams, I can't give you any kind of absolution," Platt said. "If this man comes after you, you have every right to defend yourself, friend or no friend."

"I realize that, Doc," Clint said.

"I can tell you one thing."

"What?"

"I've seen Meeker around town," the doctor said. "I've spoken to him on occasion and observed him on other occasions. If you have to face him, and you hesitate because he was once your friend . . . he's going to kill you!"

Clint studied the doctor for a few moments, then put his hand out.

"Thanks, Doc," he said, shaking the man's hand. "I think you just helped me."

"My pleasure," Platt said. "Just try not to send any business my way, if you can."

"I'll do my best, Doc."

●　●　●

When Clint left the doctor's office there was nothing left for him to do but go over to the Silver Bullet and get it over with.

What was he going to tell Meeker, though? That he should go back to his wife? Carol Meeker didn't *want* him back anymore. Why should he be trying to force them back together again?

Should he tell Meeker that this was no way to live his life? That sooner or later he'd meet a man who was better than him with a gun, and then *he'd* be the one draped over his own saddle? How many other men did Clint know who lived their lives the same way? He had never tried to talk them out of it.

Carol Meeker had written to him for help at a time when she needed it, but according to her, she no longer needed it. Hell, he'd be justified in leaving town and never coming back. Just let Jack and Carol Meeker live out the new lives they'd begun. What right did he have to even try to tell them how to live?

He was halfway to the Silver Bullet when he decided he'd have a drink there, and maybe arrange to meet with Harry that night, but in the morning he'd head back to Labyrinth, and Little Rock would no longer be on his list of future stopovers.

Chapter Thirty-Four

When he entered the saloon it was just after three in the afternoon. There were no gaming tables open and no show on the stage. There was only one girl working the room, and she wasn't Harry.

Lenny was the only bartender behind the bar. He seemed to always be the bartender when Clint was there.

"Don't you ever take a day off?" Clint said.

"That's not the way to get rich," Lenny said.

"Good point. What about your boss?"

"He's already rich," Lenny said. "He takes days off. You looking for him, Harry, . . . or Jack Meeker?"

"Is Meeker here?"

"He's upstairs with Lisa."

"Does he take very long?" Clint asked.

"Not usually," Lenny said. "At least, that's what the girls say."

"I'll have a beer."

"Sure." Lenny brought the beer and asked, "You gonna talk to him?"

"Well, if he comes down before I've finished my beer I might as well," Clint said, "even if it's only to say hello and good-bye."

"You leavin'?"

"Yep."

"Short visit this time."

"Yep."

"Comin' back?"

"I doubt it."

"In that case the beer's on the house."

"Thanks."

Clint was halfway through the beer when Jack Meeker appeared on the stairs, coming down from the second floor. When Meeker saw him standing at the bar, he stopped just for a moment, then continued on down. When he reached the bottom of the steps, he paused to hitch up his pearl-handled guns. He looked ridiculous doing it, and Clint couldn't help smiling.

"Clint," Meeker said, approaching him. He had narrowed his eyes. "I hear you're lookin' for me."

Suddenly, Clint found the whole thing very funny and couldn't conceal the fact.

"I was," Clint said, "but I'm not anymore, Jack."

"Oh? Why's that?"

"Well, I *was* going to try to talk some sense into you, but I've decided that it's your life and you should live it the way you want."

Meeker frowned at Clint and said, "Huh?"

"Never mind," Clint said, still smiling. Up close the beard and long hair looked even more ludicrous than they had out in the street.

"Is somethin' funny?" Meeker asked.

"Yeah, since you asked," Clint said, "you are. What are you dressed up for?"

"What?"

"The hair, the beard," Clint said, gesturing with his hand, "the pearl-handled guns, what's this all for, Jack? Who are you trying to be?"

Meeker looked down at himself, then around the room, at Lenny, and back at Clint.

"Somethin' wrong with the way I dress?" he asked Clint.

"It's funny, Jack," Clint said. "Don't you realize how people laugh at you when you walk past? I mean, are you *trying* to look like Bill Hickok?"

Meeker's jaw tightened as he said, "I don't think I look funny."

"Well, Jack," Clint said, putting his mug down on the bar, "you're the only one who doesn't. Look, just forget it, Jack. Have yourself a nice life—while it lasts."

"And what's that mean?" Meeker asked.

"Just that if you keep walking around trying to look like a dime novel version of a gunman, somebody's going to take you seriously and make you prove it."

"I can prove it," Meeker said. "*Anytime*, I can prove it."

"Sure, Jack," Clint said. "Good-bye." He turned and started for the door.

"Don't turn your back on me, Adams!"

Clint stopped and looked over his shoulder. Meeker had stepped away from the bar a few feet and was standing with his feet spread, his arms hanging down by his sides. There was some commotion in the room as the patrons scrambled for cover.

"You can't be serious, Jack," Clint said, turning to face the man.

"You think you're better than me, huh?" Meeker asked.

"With a gun?" Clint asked. "Jack, we *both* know I can outshoot you. Why get yourself killed trying to prove otherwise?"

"Go ahead," Meeker said, "go for your gun, Mr. Gunsmith."

"Jack," Clint said, shaking his head, "keep going after your two-hundred-dollar bounties."

With that Clint turned and walked out of the saloon. As soon as he passed through the door he stepped to the side, quickly. As he expected, Meeker came barreling out a split second later. Clint extended his leg, and Meeker tripped over it, stumbling into the street. Clint stepped down into the street and swiftly relieved the man of his guns. He tossed them into the street, where the pearl handles became covered with dirt and dust.

Meeker, not realizing that the guns were gone, came up onto his knees, reaching for them. When he realized they weren't there, he started to look around.

Clint put his foot against Meeker's chest and

pushed the man back down to the ground, where he kept him pinned. People stopped in the street to watch the altercation.

"If I wanted you dead, Jack," Clint said, "you'd be dead now. The *first* time you go up against a man who's *any* good with a gun, a man who's worth more than a two-hundred-dollar bounty, you'll be a dead man. The people of Little Rock will have to find themselves a new hero. Grow up, Jack. You're not a dime novel gunfighter; you're a rancher."

He took his foot off his former friend's chest and walked away.

"I'll get you for this, Clint!" Meeker shouted from the street. "You can't do this to me!"

Clint didn't turn. He heard Meeker shouting, "What do you think you're lookin' at? Where are my guns?"

Clint kept walking to the hotel, where he collected his gear and carried it with him to the livery. If Meeker really wanted him, he could have caught up to him by then. Maybe humiliating him in the saloon and in the street had taught the man something.

He saddled Duke and rode out of town. He wished he'd had time to say good-bye to Harry, but he wanted desperately to get out of Little Rock. His intention now was to ride out to the ranch to say good-bye to Carol, and then head back to Texas. Maybe he'd make a few stops along the way.

Chapter Thirty-Five

On the way out to the ranch Clint realized that he also had to deal with Sam Roberts. He could just talk to the young man and tell him how foolish he had been to try what he did, but Roberts *had* tried to kill him. Could he just let that go so easily? What would happen the next time some man paid attention to Carol Meeker? The next time Roberts felt his relationship with her threatened? Would he try it again and next time succeed in killing someone?

Maybe he *should* have let the sheriff deal with it. Take Roberts over to the hotel and see if the clerk could identify him. It was too late for that, though. Besides, Clint didn't need the clerk's identification. He felt sure that the shooter had been Roberts. Perhaps he should just tell Carol what happened, so she'd know that she was dealing with *another* unbalanced individual. What was it

about her that made her lean toward those types
of men?

As he rode up to the ranch he saw Toby Peters
standing at the corral. Roberts was nowhere to
be seen. Instead of riding to the house, he went
straight for the corral.

"Hello, Adams," Peters said.

"Where's Roberts?" Clint asked.

Peters turned and looked pointedly toward the
house.

"I see."

"He tried something, did he?"

Clint dismounted.

"What makes you say that?"

"He came tearing back here from town late last
night," Peters said. "Besides, you got that look on
your face."

"What look is that?"

"That you got somethin' to set right. I was tryin'
to keep an eye on him, but he got away from me
last night."

"He's not your responsibility," Clint said.

"Ah, I sort of feel like he is," Peters said. "What'd
he do, anyway?"

"He fired three shots through my door when he
thought I was standing on the other side."

"Jesus Christ," Peters said, closing his eyes.
"That would have been murder."

"That's right."

"You tell the sheriff?"

"I told him what happened," Clint said. "I didn't
tell him who it was."

"Why not?"

"I can't really prove it."

"So you came out here to take care of it yourself?" Peters asked.

"Not the way you think," Clint said, repeating what he had said to the sheriff.

"How then?"

"I'll talk to him," Clint said, "and I'll talk to Carol. She should know what she's dealing with. She doesn't need the kind of trouble Roberts can bring her."

"Maybe, if I keep an eye on him—a *closer* eye—"

"You tried that already, Peters," Clint said.

Then he looked over at the house.

"How long has he been in there?"

"About a half an hour. He went in to get somethin' to eat—so he said."

Clint looked at the man. "I've got to know where you stand," he said.

Peters rubbed his jaw. "Well, I ain't about to go up against you," he said, "and if you ain't plannin' to kill him—"

"I'm not."

Peters shrugged and said, "Then do what you got to do. I won't stand in your way."

"Fair enough," Clint said.

"What about Jack?"

"I don't know about Jack," Clint said. "I've decided that he's not my problem, any more than Roberts is yours. I'm going to talk to Carol, and then get the hell away from Little Rock."

"Don't sound like a bad idea," Peters said. "I been thinking maybe it's time for me to move on, too."

"With the kid?"

"I guess that depends on what happens in the next ten minutes, don't it?"

"Might as well get it over with," Clint said.

"I'll watch your horse."

"Thanks."

Clint had no doubt that Peters was going to keep his distance. Jack Meeker notwithstanding, he was usually a pretty good judge of character. Toby Peters hadn't reached his age by taking a hand in somebody else's game if he didn't have to. He'd stay right where he was and see how things played out, and then he'd decide what to do with his own life.

Clint walked toward the house, not even sure if he was just going to walk in or knock first. He didn't know what was going on inside, but he wanted to get this over with fast. He decided that the best thing to do was enter unannounced. There was no point in giving Roberts another chance to succeed now where he had failed last night.

He mounted the front porch and hit the door without breaking stride.

Carol Meeker and Sam Roberts were sitting at the table, with a meal spread out in front of them.

"Clint—" Carol said, starting to get to her feet.

Roberts turned, saw who it was, then looked at his gun, which was hanging on the chair next to him.

"Don't!" Clint shouted.

Chapter Thirty-Six

Of course, it wouldn't have taken much for Clint to simply draw and fire, killing the younger man before he reached his gun, but he didn't *want* to kill the kid, in spite of the fact that the man had already tried to kill him.

Instead of pulling his gun he followed the man's movement, staying right behind him. He reached Roberts as Roberts reached his gun. The man grabbed his gun and started to turn, but was met with Clint's boot, which knocked the gun cleanly from his hand.

"Don't be stupid," he said, but Roberts wasn't listening.

He stood up straight and swung at Clint, who ducked under the blow, stepped inside its arc, and hit Roberts in the abdomen. The blow drove the air from the man's lungs and stunned him. Clint decided to follow up and hit Roberts a blow to the jaw, which sat him down on the floor—hard!

"Clint!" Carol Meeker cried out.

"It's all right, Carol," Clint said, putting his hand out to stop her from protesting any further. "I'm done if he is."

Roberts was on the floor, his head swimming from the blow to the jaw, still trying to draw air into his lungs from the blow to the abdomen. He held his hand up to Clint and sort of wiggled it in the air, which Clint took as a gesture that he *had* had enough.

Clint gave Roberts time to catch his breath and get himself together by walking over and picking up the fallen gun. He tucked it into his belt, turned, and waited for Roberts to be ready to talk.

"Clint," Carol said, confused, "what's going on?"

"Your young Lothario, here, tried to kill me yesterday," Clint said.

"What?" Carol asked.

"I—I—" Roberts said.

"He knocked on my door and then fired several shots through it when he thought I was standing in front of it," Clint said. "Not the most courageous act I've ever witnessed."

"Why?" she said, looking down at Roberts, who was still helplessly trying to speak. She turned her attention to Clint and asked, "Why would he do that?"

"Because he was jealous."

"Jealous?"

"Of us."

"Of us?" She was confused and repeating everything he said.

"He thinks you're going to get rid of him in favor of a relationship with me," Clint said.

Carol looked down at Roberts and asked, "How could you?"

Roberts had finally drawn enough air to restore his breathing and his ability to speak.

"I didn't—" he said.

"You can finally speak, and you're going to lie?" Clint asked. "Come on, you were seen running from the hotel, kid. Don't bother denying this."

Roberts turned and glowered at Clint.

"I suppose you told the sheriff?" he said, still rubbing his abdomen. He might have been trying to play Carol for some sympathy, but Clint felt they were beyond that now.

"No, I didn't."

Roberts frowned and said, "You didn't?"

"Oh, I told him someone shot at me, but I didn't tell him who it was."

"Why not?" Carol asked.

"I just thought I could handle the situation myself," Clint said.

"That means you're gonna kill me," Roberts said.

"No," Clint said, "if I were going to do that, you'd be dead already."

"What are you gonna do, then?" Roberts asked.

"Why did you come here?" Carol asked.

"I came first to say good-bye to you," he said. "I'm leaving."

"Leaving?" she asked. "Already? Have you seen Jack yet?"

"I have," Clint said, "and we settled nothing. I just don't think there's anything I can do for him, Carol. He's going to have to learn the errors of his new life-style himself. The other reason I came was to see Roberts, here, and make sure he realizes he did the wrong thing in trying to kill me." He looked at Carol and added, "I also wanted to make sure that you knew what he did."

At that point Roberts worked his way to his feet and stood facing Clint and Carol.

"Carol," he said, "let me explain."

"Explain what?" she demanded. "Why you tried to kill a man I regard as a good friend?"

"I'm sorry," Roberts said. "I—I was jealous. I didn't know what I was doing—"

"That's no excuse for trying to kill somebody," she said. "Sam . . . please leave."

"Leave?"

"Yes," she said. "You're fired."

"Fired?" he repeated in disbelief. "Carol, you can't mean that?"

"I do mean it," she said. "I want you to pack your things and get off my property."

"Carol!" Roberts said, looking aghast. "You can't mean it! I thought we had—"

"I'm sorry, Sam," Carol said, wrapping her arms around herself tightly. "I do mean it."

Roberts stared at Carol for a few moments, but when she refused to look at him anymore he picked up his hat and started for the door.

When he reached it he turned around and looked at Clint.

"My gun?"

Clint took the man's gun out of his belt, ejected the shells from it, and tossed it to him. Roberts caught it clumsily and then left the house.

"Should you let him go?" Carol asked. "I mean, he tried to kill you."

"I can understand how he felt, Carol," Clint said, even though he really couldn't understand it. "I think maybe you should rethink your new life-style as well."

"Mine?" Carol asked. "What else am I supposed to do when my husband *left* me—and not for another woman, but for *killing* people."

"I don't know, Carol," Clint said. "I don't think I can help you any more than I can help Jack. The two of you are going to have to live your own lives. I'm not going to try to interfere with your lives any further."

He started for the door, and she called after him, "Clint—"

"I'm sorry, Carol," he said. "I *have* to say good-bye this time."

He walked out of the house without looking back.

Chapter Thirty-Seven

As Clint left the house he saw Toby Peters standing by the corral and walked over to talk to him.

"She threw him out, huh?" Peters asked.

"I'm afraid so," Clint said. "She fired him. I'm sorry."

Peters waved away Clint's apology.

"It's his own fault . . . isn't it?"

"Yes, it is," Clint said. "Where did he go?"

"I expect he's packin' his gear."

"What about you? Will you stay when he leaves?"

Peters hesitated and then shrugged.

"I guess I'll talk to Mrs. Meeker and see what she wants to do," Peters said. "What about you? Where are you headin' now?"

"I'm leavin'," Clint said. "I'm finished meddling in the lives of these two people. They'll have to go on without me now."

"Can't say I blame you," Peters said.

"Good luck to you, Peters," Clint said, and the two men shook hands.

Clint climbed up onto Duke's back and rode away. He intended to circle around the town of Little Rock so he wouldn't have to ride through it again and then continue on back to Texas.

Several hours later Clint had successfully bypassed Little Rock, but because he was riding in a wide semicircle to avoid it, he had not actually put a lot of miles between himself and town. He was sort of mentally wishing the town farewell when he heard the first shot. By the time he actually heard the shot, the bullet had already passed him. He was in the air, having launched himself from the saddle, by the time the second bullet whizzed by and the sound of the shot reached him.

"Son of a bitch!" Clint cried out as he hit the ground. He was scolding himself for letting Sam Roberts off the hook so easily. He just didn't think that the kid would come after him and try to ambush him.

He found cover behind a small knoll and waited for more shots to come, but they did not. He lifted his head slowly, to see if anyone would try to shoot it off, and when no more shots were forthcoming he actually stood up. When there were still no more shots he brushed himself off and started walking to recover Duke.

He had probably been foolish not to tell Sheriff Hays about Roberts, but he was going to remedy that right now. One more trip into Little Rock, then, to talk to the sheriff so that he wouldn't have to be looking over his shoulder all the way to Texas.

Chapter Thirty-Eight

As he entered Little Rock he was wondering
about Sam Roberts, and whether or not it actually
was that young man who had just tried to bushwhack him. He had given Jack Meeker enough of
a reason to want to kill him, so it might have been
Meeker who tried to shoot him from his horse a
little while ago.

Were there any others in town he had given
some motive to? He couldn't see Ken Becker
sending someone after him again, as he had
done the last time Clint was in town. He and
the saloon owner didn't really have a bone of
contention between them anymore.

He rode right up to the sheriff's office and dismounted. His experience had been such that he
expected the sheriff to be behind his desk when he
entered, drinking coffee or going through posters,

so he was surprised to find that the man was not there at all.

Instead of waiting for the sheriff to come back, he decided to go and look for him. The quicker he spoke to the lawman, the faster he could be on his way once again and put Little Rock behind him for good.

Outside he decided to leave Duke where he was, in front of the sheriff's office, and walk around town on foot looking for the man.

After an hour he still hadn't found Hays, but he did find himself in front of the Silver Bullet. He decided to go in for a drink.

The place was pretty busy, but he found a space at the bar and signaled Lenny that he wanted a beer.

"Thought you'd be on your way," Lenny said, putting the beer on the bar in front of him.

"So did I," Clint said, lifting the mug. "Turns out I still have some business with the sheriff. When I get that done I will be on my way."

"You'll have to wait for him to come back into town, then," Lenny said.

"Oh? Where'd he go?"

"Just north of town," Lenny said. "Somebody came riding in sayin' they found a dead body. He went out to take a look at it."

"A dead body?" Clint said, very interested. "Who was it?"

The bartender shrugged.

"That's what he went out there to find out."

"Have you seen Meeker?" Clint asked.

"Not since he was here with you," Lenny said.

Clint wondered about the body and whether it had anything to do with his situation.

"North of town, you say?" he asked.

"Just north of town, yeah."

Clint finished the beer and said, "Thanks for the information, Lenny."

"Be back this way again?" Lenny asked.

"I doubt it."

"Good luck, then."

He started for the door and turned when he heard his name. It was Harry coming toward him.

"Leaving without saying good-bye again?" she asked him.

"I'm sorry, Harry," he said. "Things have been so messed up—"

"I understand," she said. "I really do. I just thought you were gone already, and I'm grateful for the chance to say good-bye."

She looked around, then gave a hell-with-it shrug and reached up and kissed him shortly.

"I'm sorry . . ." he said again, somewhat helplessly. He wished he did have the time and the inclination to say good-bye to her in a more leisurely way.

He left the saloon and hurried to where he had left Duke.

Chapter Thirty-Nine

Clint rode north of town, aware of the fact that if he rode far enough north he'd come to the Meeker ranch again. He didn't think he'd get that far, though, and he turned out to be right.

Well before he would have reached the Meeker place he saw the sheriff and a couple of other men loading a body onto a buckboard. Sheriff Hays looked around as he rode up to the scene.

"Adams," Hays said. "I thought you'd be gone by now."

"So did I," Clint said, dismounting. "I had something to talk to you about before I left, though."

"We can talk when I get back to town," Hays said.

"What have you got here?"

"A dead body," Hays said. He started to turn away, then stopped and looked at Clint again. From the look on the man's face Clint knew he was going to be asked a lawman-type question.

"What is it?" Clint asked.

"This might actually turn out to be something you know about," Hays said. "Did you go out to the Meeker ranch to see Mrs. Meeker, like you said you were going to do?"

"Sure," Clint said. "I was there briefly, and then I left to go back to Texas."

"And then came back, huh?"

"Right."

"To talk to me."

"Right."

"About what?"

"I thought we were going to talk about it back in town," Clint said.

"Just answer the question."

"Somebody took a shot at me."

"Again?"

"That's right."

"Think it was the same person?"

"Well, I did, originally," Clint said.

"What changed your mind?"

"I don't know," Clint said. "I just didn't think it would be something he'd pull."

"Who are we talking about?"

"That's what I wanted to talk to you about," Clint said. "The man who shot through my door was Sam Roberts. Do you know who he is?"

"He works for Mrs. Meeker, doesn't he?"

"That's right."

"Why would he want to kill you?"

"Jealousy."

Hays frowned and said, "I don't think I want to hear any more about that. So you don't think he took a shot at you this second time?"

"I'm just saying that there's somebody else who might have wanted to do it."

"Meeker himself, you mean?"

"Yes."

"Also out of jealousy?"

"No," Clint said. "I was kind of hard on him at the saloon earlier today."

"I heard about that."

"It's getting dark," Clint said. "Shouldn't we head back to town?"

"I guess you're gonna have to stay around another day after all, huh? Can't leave in the dark."

"I guess," Clint said.

"Maybe before we go back you should take a look at something."

"What?"

Hays waved him over to the buckboard. Clint approached as Hays removed the blanket that was covering the dead body.

"Do you know him?"

Clint turned his head to get a good look at the dead man.

"Yeah," he said, with a sinking sensation in his stomach, "I know him."

"Who was he?"

"You know who he was," Clint said. "Sam Roberts."

"The man who worked for Mrs. Meeker?"

"Right."

"And the one who tried to kill you in your hotel room?"

"That's right."

"Did you and him have a problem out at Mrs. Meeker's today?"

Clint frowned, wondering if Hays had already talked to Carol Meeker about that. He decided not to lie. There was no reason to.

"Yes, we had an . . . altercation," Clint said. "I kept him from shooting me."

"And then what?"

"Carol Meeker fired him and ran him off the ranch."

"Adams," Hays said, "did you do this?"

"No, Sheriff," Clint said, evenly, "I didn't kill him. I had no reason to."

"He tried to kill you."

"A lot of people have," Clint said. "I told Carol what had happened, and she fired him. That was the end of it as far as I was concerned."

"I see," Hays said. He dropped the blanket back over the dead man's face. "Look, if he came after you, and you had to kill him, I'll understand that."

Chapter Forty

Clint rode back to town with Hays and the men with the buckboard. When they got there, the other men took the body to the undertaker's while Clint and Hays went looking for Meeker. He still appeared to be out of town. They went back to the sheriff's office to discuss the situation over coffee.

"Maybe he went out to the ranch," Clint said.

"Why would he do that?"

"I don't know," Clint said. "Maybe he figured that's where I'd go."

"But if he took that shot at you, then he was south of town a couple of hours ago. That wouldn't give him time to get back to the ranch."

"If he started right after he took the shots at me, he might be there by now."

"And by the time we get there, he could be gone," Hays said.

"You're probably right," Clint said. "Besides, it's dark now. I guess we just have to wait for him to come back to town."

"That may not be until tomorrow," Hays pointed out. "You'll be leavin' in the mornin', won't you?"

"I don't know about that," Clint said. "There's been a killing now and another attempt on my life. I'd sort of like to find out who's behind it."

"You'd like to know if it's Meeker, huh?"

"Well, sure," Clint said, "wouldn't you like to find out if a man you once thought of as a friend was now trying to kill you?"

"I guess I would," Hays said. "Do you think he killed Roberts?"

"I don't know."

"If he didn't," Hays said, "then I've got a killer runnin' loose around here—that is, unless you want to change what you told me earlier."

"Believe me," Clint said, "I was telling you the truth. I didn't kill Sam Roberts."

"Okay," Hays said, "I accept that."

Clint stood up.

"Where are you goin'?"

"If I'm going to stay, I'll have to take care of my horse and get a hotel room again," Clint said. At the door he paused and said, "Why is it I can't seem to get away from this place?"

"Maybe it's because there's still unfinished business to take care of," Hays suggested.

"I guess you're right, Sheriff," Clint said. "I'll see you later."

"I'll be at the Silver Bullet later," Hays said. "I'll buy you a drink."

"I'll be there."

Chapter Forty-One

The only good thing about having to come back to Little Rock was that Clint would get an opportunity to say a proper good-bye to Harry. She lit up the saloon with a smile when he walked in, then she led him to an empty table. He had dinner there and was nursing an after-dinner beer when Sheriff Hays walked in.

"Started without me, I see," Hays said, sitting down opposite Clint.

"I had dinner," Clint said, and then raising the half-empty mug added, "This is my first."

"All right," Hays said, "the second one is on me, then."

He turned to see if any of the girls were nearby, but Harry was way ahead of him. She was already on her way to the table with two beers.

"Thanks, Harry," Clint said.

"These are on me, Harry," Hays said.

"Sure, Sheriff." She gave Clint a dazzling smile and went back to work.

"Any new developments?" Clint asked.

Hays took a healthy pull on his beer and then said, "None." He licked foam from his lips and set the mug down on the table. "I'll have to talk to Mrs. Meeker tomorrow morning. Maybe she can tell me whether or not this Roberts fella had a run-in with anyone else lately."

"Like her husband?"

"Maybe."

"You might also talk to a fella name of Toby Peters," Clint said. "He *was* working for Carol out there. I don't know if he stayed after she fired Roberts."

"I know Toby," Hays said. "If he's not out there, I'll know where to find him. He and the kid pretty close?"

"Peters seemed to have taken him under his wing," Clint said. "I don't think he approved of what was going on between Carol and Roberts."

"Tell me again what happened between you and Meeker?" Hays asked.

Clint explained how Meeker seemed to want to brace him, and how he refused. Finally, he related how he had taken Meeker's guns away from him and humiliated him in the street.

"Well," Hays said, "that's reason enough for him to want to kill you, all right, but I can't see where he'd have reason to kill Roberts."

"Unless he found out about Roberts and his wife."

"But why would he care?" Hays asked. "He left his wife; he's been cattin' around with Becker's stable."

"Yeah," Clint said, "but she's still his wife, Sheriff."

"I guess you're right," Hays said. He finished his beer and put the empty mug down on the table.

"Another?" Clint asked. "On me this time?"

"No," Hays said, "one's my limit. I usually have it about this time of night. I've got to go out and make my rounds."

"See you in the morning, then."

Hays stood up, but seemed reluctant to leave.

"Look," he said, "I'm sort of committed to takin' a ride out to the Meeker place to talk to Mrs. Meeker tomorrow mornin'."

"What about it?"

"Well, that'll leave you here in town," Hays said, "and Meeker might show up."

"What do you want me to do?"

"I'm not sure," Hays said.

"Want me to promise I won't kill him until you get to talk to him?"

"He may not give you much of a choice if he sees you," Hays said, "and I guess you're gonna brace him about whether or not he tried to bushwhack you." It was more of a statement than a question.

"I'm going to ask him about it, yeah."

"Ask him . . ."

"Sheriff," Clint said, "I can only promise you one thing."

"What's that?"

"I'm not going to shoot him on sight."

Hays frowned, then sighed and said, "I guess that's all I can ask for."

Clint remained at the Silver Bullet through Danielle Becker's performance. It occurred to him then that he didn't know what her surname had been before she married Ken Becker. It also occurred to him that he didn't much care.

What he was thinking about mostly was the death of a friend. It was bad enough having to suffer the death of a friend once, but there was a distinct possibility that he would have to suffer the death of Jack Meeker twice.

As far as he was concerned the Jack Meeker who had been his friend for twelve years was already gone, as good as dead. Now, if Meeker was the one who had tried to bushwhack him, it was not only possible that Meeker would die for real, but that Clint would be the one to kill him.

At this point, whether Meeker lived or died was entirely up to him. Clint would not give the man another chance at his back. If Meeker wanted to try to kill him, he was going to have to do it face-to-face.

"Wanna get out of here?" Harry asked.

He hadn't heard her approach the table, but he was glad she had.

"Yes," he said, "very much."

"Come on, sad man," she said, taking his arm and pulling him to his feet. "I'll take you to your hotel and cheer you up."

And he had no doubt that she could do it, too.

Chapter Forty-Two

Clint was awakened the next morning by an incessant pounding on his door. Harry was stirring next to him as he staggered to his feet, pulled on his pants, and went to the door to answer it. He was surprised when he opened it to find Carol Meeker standing there. She looked frightened and not a little bedraggled. She had obviously come a long way in a short period of time and seemed out of breath.

"Thank God you're still here," she said.

"Carol, what is it?"

"Let me in."

"Carol . . ." he said, protesting.

She pushed past him and stopped short when she saw Harry sitting up in bed. When Harry saw her, she pulled the sheet up to cover herself, but she did it slowly.

Carol turned to Clint and for a moment he

thought he was going to have to deal with some female righteous indignation, but that wasn't the case.

"Jack's gone crazy!"

"What do you mean?"

"He killed Sam Roberts."

"How do you know that?"

"He told me."

"When?"

"Last night," she said. "He came to the house, told me he killed Roberts, and that he was going to kill you next. Then he stayed. He—he made me stay with him all night. He—he raped me. When I woke up this morning he was asleep, and I sneaked out."

Behind her Harry had slid from the bed and was getting dressed.

"Was the sheriff out there this morning?" Clint asked.

"I didn't see him," she said. "Why?"

"He was coming out there to talk to you," Clint said.

"Clint, if he surprises Jack, Jack will kill him," Carol said quickly.

From behind, Harry put her hands on Carol's shoulders to comfort her.

"You go ahead, Clint," Harry said. "I'll take care of her."

"Jesus," Carol said, tears rolling down her face, "he's really gone crazy this time, Clint. Be careful, or he'll kill you, too."

"I'll be back as soon as I can," Clint said. He

hastily pulled on his boots, donned a shirt, and buckled his gun belt on. "Stay here with her, Harry."

"I'll take her over to the doctor's," Harry said, "and then get her a bath and some clean clothes. We'll be here when you get back, Clint."

"Thanks."

Carol was silently weeping, and as Clint went out the door he heard Harry saying, "It'll be okay, honey. . . ."

He didn't think she was necessarily going to be right.

Clint pushed Duke to the limit in his haste to get out to the Meeker ranch, but he had a sense of dread the entire way. If Jack Meeker was crazy enough to confess to murder and then rape his own wife, then there wasn't anything he wouldn't do— and that included killing a lawman. Once again, as he had done in the past, Clint couldn't help but wonder where *this* Jack Meeker had come from, where he had been hiding all these years.

When he reached the ranch his sense of dread was immediately realized. There was a man lying on the ground in front of the house. If it was Jack Meeker then it was all over, but he didn't think so.

He reined Duke in hard and dismounted before the animal had even come to a full stop. He ran to the man and turned him over. It was Sheriff Hays, and he had a wound in his left side. The bullet had gone in low, and if it had traveled straight then it had missed his heart. The man's eyes fluttered and opened.

"Jesus," he said.

"Take it easy."

"I didn't have a chance," Hays said. "I was walking up to the house when the door opened and Meeker fired. He—he never even warned me."

"Take it easy," Clint said, examining the wound. "It doesn't look too bad. I think you'll make it."

"I'll be all right," Hays said. "You've got to get back to town. He said he was gonna kill his own wife, and then he was going after you."

"Shit," Clint said. What should he do now? Leave Hays and go after Meeker before he could get to Carol, or get Hays some help first?

"Clint," Hays said, "pack the wound to stop the bleeding and then go. I'll be all right."

"Come on," Clint said, putting Hays's left arm around his neck, "I'll get you into the house, patch you up, and then I'll get back to town."

"Y-you might not make it," Hays said as Clint dragged him to his feet.

"Don't worry," Clint said. "I'll make it."

Chapter Forty-Three

In addition to Duke's speed Clint had always admired the big, black gelding's stamina. If it hadn't been for that, there would have been no way the animal could have carried him back to Little Rock so quickly. His big partner deserved a good rest and feed after that morning's work.

As he rode back into Little Rock he was surprised to find the streets empty. Even this early there was usually some signs of life in any town. Before he could wonder what was going on, though, he heard the shots and knew what it must be.

He reined Duke in and dismounted, allowing the horse to move off out of harm's way. He could hear the shots, but he couldn't see where they were coming from. They were not being directed at him.

Leaving his gun in his holster he moved along

179

the main street, following the sound of the shots. Soon, he was also able to hear a man shouting. Finally, he saw Jack Meeker. The man was running across the street, shouting, then running back across the other way.

"Carol, where are you?" he was calling. "Damn it, I'll find you, you bitch! You can't run out on me like that!"

Jesus, Clint thought, who ran out on who, Jack? He'd left his wife behind a long time ago, and now he was angry because the morning after he raped her she ran away from him?

"Carol!" Meeker shouted. "Come out! I killed one of your boyfriends, and after I'm finished with you, I'm gonna kill your other one, Clint Adams. My *friend!*"

Clint was surprised at the bitterness in Meeker's voice. It was as if the man actually *believed* that he was the aggrieved party.

Clint decided to move out into the middle of the street and wait for Meeker to notice him.

Meeker kept zigzagging across the street until he spotted Clint. Then he stopped short and turned to face him. There was a fair distance of ground separating them, so he also took the time to reload his guns, and then holster them.

"Where you been, Clint?" he called out. "I thought you would've come out of hidin' a long time ago."

"I was out at the ranch, Jack," Clint said. "I found Hays."

"Yeah, that was too bad," Meeker said, "but he

didn't give me much of a choice. I had to kill him."

"Well, you didn't," Clint said, taking a few slow steps toward the man.

"What?"

"He's still alive, and he's going to arrest you as soon as he gets back to town."

"For what?"

"For killing Sam Roberts—which I just heard you confess to—and for shooting him. He might also throw in rape."

"Who am I supposed to have raped?"

"Carol."

Meeker laughed.

"She's my *wife*."

The man had a point. Unfortunately, that charge might not stick according to the law, but as far as Clint was concerned the man had committed rape. Clint considered rape a coward's crime.

"That doesn't matter, Jack," Clint said. "You raped her, and that's the act of a coward. You also shot Hays down without warning. Another cowardly act."

"Are you callin' me a coward?"

"I thought I was being very clear about that," Clint said. "If not, let me make it real clear for you." Clint shouted at the top of his lungs so the whole town could hear him. "Jack Meeker is a dirty coward!"

"You son of a bitch!" Meeker said. "You think I don't know about you and my wife?"

"You left your wife a long time ago, Jack," Clint

said. "She had to try to build a life of her own."

"With you? With that punk, Roberts?"

"With whoever she wanted."

"I'm gonna kill you, Clint."

"That's a shame, Jack," Clint said. "We used to be friends."

"We were never friends," Meeker said. "You always thought you was better than me. You always wanted my wife."

"You're crazy, Jack," Clint said. "You're stark raving mad, and I tell you what. Killing you will be a pleasure. It will be like killing a mad dog. Now come on, let's get it over with. Show this town you're not a coward. Go for those pretty pearl-handled guns so I can kill you fair and square."

"You ain't gonna kill me," Meeker said, "I'm gonna kill you."

"Then do it," Clint said.

Clint had been moving slowly toward Meeker the whole time and was now close enough to see the indecision on the man's face.

"I'll put two bullets in you before you even clear leather, Jack," Clint said slowly, "and you know it."

Meeker was flexing his hands and licking his lips. The perspiration was coming down so heavily that it was dripping from his chin to the ground, forming a damp spot.

"Now, Jack. Now!"

Whether he intended to or not, Meeker jumped at the sound of Clint's voice, and his hands moved for his guns.

Clint was surprised at how easy it was. Not that he hadn't expected to outdraw Meeker. He had. No, it was that it was so easy to pull the trigger that amazed him. Maybe it was the rape, or the shooting of Hays, that was the last straw. Whatever it was, Clint felt that the world would be a better place without Jack Meeker, and so he cleanly outdrew the man and calmly put two bullets in his chest before Meeker could clear leather with his pretty guns.

As promised.

**Speaking Volumes
is proud to announce a
New Adult Western Series**

Coming Spring 2017

By
AWARD-WINNING AUTHOR
J.R. Roberts

Roxanne Louise Doyle is Lady Gunsmith,
a hot, sexy woman who is unmatched with a gun…

A Speaking Volumes Original Publication

**For more information
visit: www.speakingvolumes.us**

ANGEL EYES *series*
by
Award-Winning Author
Robert J. Randisi (J.R. Roberts)

Visit us at <u>www.speakingvolumes.us</u>

TRACKER *series*
by
Award-Winning Author
Robert J. Randisi (J.R. Roberts)

Visit us at www.speakingvolumes.us

MOUNTAIN JACK PIKE *series*
by
Award-Winning Author
Robert J. Randisi (J.R. Roberts)

Visit us at www.speakingvolumes.us

Sign up for free and bargain books

Join the Speaking Volumes mailing list

Text

ILOVEBOOKS

to 22828 **to get started.**

Printed in Great Britain
by Amazon

40447382R00111